Also by MARLY YOUMANS

The Curse of the Raven Mocker

INGLEDOVE

INGLEDOVE

MARLY YOUMANS

Farrar Straus Giroux ⟫ New York

Copyright © 2005 by Marly Youmans
Illustration copyright © 2005 by Renato Alarcão
All rights reserved
Distributed in Canada by Douglas & McIntyre Publishing Group
Printed in the United States of America
Designed by Nancy Goldenberg
First edition, 2005
1   3   5   7   9   10   8   6   4   2

www.fsgkidsbooks.com

Library of Congress Cataloging-in-Publication Data
Youmans, Marly.
  Ingledove / Marly Youmans.— 1st ed.
    p.   cm.
  Summary: Several years after Fontana dam flooded the town where they
were born, Ingledove and her brother Lang go wandering in the southern
Appalachians, where they encounter their mother's peculiar people, the
Adantans, and an evil being who charms Lang.
  ISBN-13: 978-0-374-33599-1
  ISBN-10: 0-374-33599-0
  [1. Supernatural—Fiction.   2. Voyages and travels—Fiction.   3. Brothers
and sisters—Fiction.   4. Mountain life—Appalachian Region—Fiction.
5. Appalachian Region—History—20th century—Fiction.]   I. Title.

PZ7.Y843In   2005
[Fic]—dc22

2004047188

For Benjamin Francis Miller

I watched the water-snakes:
They moved in tracks of shining white,
And when they reared, the elfish light
Fell off in hoary flakes.

Within the shadow of the ship
I watched their rich attire:
Blue, glossy green, and velvet black,
They coiled and swam; and every track
Was a flash of golden fire.

O happy living things! no tongue
Their beauty might declare:
A spring of love gushed from my heart,
And I blessed them unaware.

—SAMUEL TAYLOR COLERIDGE
The Rime of the Ancient Mariner

CONTENTS

Ingledove

NIGHT SORCERY

Danagasta was the one who had suggested the trip to Hazel Creek, who told them how to get from Bryson City to the spot where the rowboat was hidden under a heap of brush. No mother would have urged such an adventure, but Danagasta was no mother. She mentioned the idea twice or more before Lang took the bait. Now here they were in deep waters.

Ingledove remembered resisting her brother's decision. It had seemed unwise, somehow, frightening to go on the train without anyone else along, then to hire a wagon and at the end to walk to a secret place where the boat was hidden.

"Did you leave it there? How do you know?" she had asked.

The woman had sucked on her pipe stem and then yawned, letting smoke obscure her face. When she spoke, her words were in proper English and seemed guarded, though she continued to rock and nurse her tobacco as usual.

"Maybe I did. Maybe I just remember. Maybe. But you'll

go, mind, and you'll wander farther than you meant. The pair of you." Her lids had drooped over her eyes as she said, "It's meant for you to go. Intended."

Ingledove had drawn back, considering. The old lady was getting stiff in her body and mind, she had thought.

"That is," Danagasta had gone on in a lower voice, "the journey was foretold. But who knows what will come of it? The boy is wild, wild. They're both wild at the heart. And I don't know what will be demanded."

The wrinkles below her eyes were moist, though Ingledove had never before seen her shed a tear.

"Well, you must row over the drowned lands to the high hills where your marm was born, and I must stay and wait," she had declared, the words and the pipe in her fingers lending her the air of a judge with gavel, pronouncing sentence. "Before she passed, Pearly cried and said that she would never get home again, and she begged me to send you there. Someday maybe you'll know what she meant. Your marm broke with her folks and made her bed with an outlander, and she bided with her choosing. She was the last of her line, and after a while there wasn't any home left but with you two. That and waiting for a man who never came home."

The woman had dug in her pipe with a twig and then rapped it against the garden gate, knocking out crumbs of dottle.

"Now it's time to pay your respects to the graves of your mother and of the little children who have gone on growing in the next world. That's all. Just as simple as that." She had put out her hand, and the girl had taken it, feeling the dry smooth palm against hers.

"Jest a nervish dummern," she had added, reverting to the oldest sort of mountain talk.

"Not you."

But Danagasta had proved to be a nervous woman the night before they left, when a scream rent the midnight peace of the Copper Baron's house. Ingledove sat bolt upright in the bed, hugging the coverlet. Moonlight fell in splotches on the floor, filtered through the cucumber tree outside the windows. In a minute she heard the sound of slapping feet—Danagasta's slippers, passing along the great square opening in the immense hall, through which one could see the landing and the stairs below and the bold checkering of the lower hall. In a moment, she poked her head through the door, lifting the lantern she liked to carry at night. The leaping flame of the candle threw a grotesque swinging profile on the wall, and Ingledove pressed the sheets against her mouth.

"Was that you? Get out of bed! Come on, now." She looked paler than the girl had ever seen her. The lantern trembled in her hand.

They padded down the hallway, the young one clutching the border of the old one's shawl for reassurance. The two stopped on the doorsill of Lang's room, its depths partly lit by moonlight.

"He's a-thrashing." Danagasta's voice was hushed.

The pair drew nearer the bed, where the boy seemed caught by coils of sheeting. In his nightmare he had twisted until the cloth had become ropes around his legs and a tight restraint across his chest. Ingledove shivered, seeing the whites of his eyes between his barely open lids. Pinpricks of moisture dotted his arms and neck, and beads of sweat stood on his forehead. A muscle in his throat was visible, pulled taut. She could hear his teeth grinding, a low desperate noise.

"Wake him." She pressed against the shawl.

"It's night sorcery," the other whispered; she hesitated, hand out, then let it brush against his shoulder. Lang let out a howl as he wrestled with the covers. Strange to see him throw his head from side to side as he muttered syllables they could not make out.

"Lang," the woman soothed, "Lang, Lang, it's all right."

He slowed, as if he had heard something, and then to Ingledove's great surprise, tears rolled down his face. Or maybe it was only sweat; he never cried, not even when he had been injured at games or fallen from the basswood with its ramshackle tree house. It was even more shocking than the idea that Danagasta might weep.

Now the two of them called the sleeper's name, reeling him from the deeps of slumber.

He responded incoherently, loudly, and just before he woke let out a series of hoarse shouts. The perspiration poured from him as his eyelids flung open, and he stared unblinking into the dark.

"It's me, Lang, it's me," Ingledove blurted out. She had lurched backward when his eyes flew open, as if the fierce gaze could hurt her.

"Calm down, son." The old woman rested a hand on his cheek. He kept on staring until his eyes seemed to find something familiar in his sister's face.

"The night rider caught you," Danagasta said softly, beginning to unravel the covers and loosen them from around the bare chest. That was always her answer to a nightmare—the wizard who would mount the sleeper and ride.

Lang shook his head violently and seized her by the arm.

"I dreamed . . ." he began, then stopped to rub the drops from his lashes and blot his face with the bed sheets.

"What did you see?" she prompted. Dreams were important to Danagasta. She would listen to a long recital from a child in complete patience, and afterward she would interpret the dream "by her lights."

He gazed at a point across the room. It appeared that he might perceive something lurking there, invisible to others. He paid no attention as she continued to unwind the twisted bedclothes from his legs.

"I heard," he said slowly, "a voice. And in my dream it pleased me more than any I'd known before. It told me about myself, said that I was vain but deserved self-love. That careless ways were easy and pleasant. That I rushed into things with no thought for danger. The words were like a song, peculiar and bewitching. They had a bell-like quality."

He tilted his head slightly to one side as if listening for notes. Danagasta waited.

"What then?" Ingledove asked. She glanced uneasily over one shoulder and sank onto the foot of the bed.

"I came to a big palace. It looked like this house a little, because the windows had diamond panes. I went inside and walked a long way through white halls with only an occasional chair set against the wall or a door. But I didn't stop. I kept on until the floor fell away into a ravine. On the other side was a drawbridge, the wood bolted with golden nails. It slammed down in front of me, and I walked across."

Ingledove turned and surveyed the part of the room where he kept staring, as if trying to penetrate its recesses.

"In the middle of a huge chamber was a well, with blood-stained shirts draped on its edge. I could hear the voice, so lovely, laughing in the background. There was a rustling sound, and in flowed a white snake, its head reared up high as a man."

The girl looked at her brother, his eyes bright.

"I don't know what happened afterward, except that I was tangled in coils and couldn't get out. And it bit me. Right here." He slid a hand along his chest, stopping just below the collarbone.

Danagasta clicked her tongue against the roof of her mouth. It was a signal of disturbance both children knew well.

"Scratched by a briar," she said quietly, then stood without speaking for a while, until she nodded, decisive at last. "Get up," she ordered.

Lang swung his legs around and stood, reaching out a hand to steady himself.

"Now help me move this bed," she commanded.

What did she mean to do? When the others lifted it from the corner, Ingledove bent over and peered under the frame, half expecting to see a reptile curled in sleep.

"Lie down again." Danagasta patted the pillow, and Lang obeyed.

Setting the lantern among the schoolbooks on the boy's writing table, she spat on her hand and smeared the saliva on his skin at the spot he had indicated. Then she began to sing a plaintive tune:

Dunuwa, dunuwa, dunuwa,
Dunuwa, dunuwa, dunuwa.
A baby rabbit nipped your chest.
Dayuha, dayuha, dayuha,
Dayuha, dayuha—
A salamander marked your breast.

Shuffling in her slippers, she moved slowly to the left, circling the bedstead, pausing now and then to rub the place where the dream snake had bitten. As Lang watched her dance, he seemed to relax, and at last amusement crossed his face. But Ingledove did not like it, not the gloom that had drawn her dreamer's glance or the weird rays from the candle lantern or the strange words.

Dunuwa, dunuwa, dunuwa,
Dunuwa, dunuwa, dunuwa.
A climbing froglet kissed your skin.
Dayuha, dayuha, dayuha,
Dayuha, dayuha—
A tiny bug pricked like a pin.

At the end, Lang laughed. "What was that, old witch?" He tugged at her shawl. "What was all that?"

In the beams of candlelight she looked grim and sour.

"Your mother knew the difference between a witch and a master of a witch, even if you don't know any better. There's evil that has ways to see and snatch at you from its caves in the mountains. You don't uncoil that snake, you'll find yourself dying, pretty boy," she cautioned, drawing herself to full height. "Maybe not tonight, maybe not this year, or this ten years. But sure as you were born of a woman, death will come sniffing and the bite fester if you don't unwind the snake."

He stopped laughing, though he still had a faint smile at his lips. The two of them exchanged a long look, and at last he nodded, as if bowing to her authority.

"Snakes coil to the right, do they?" he observed aloud, not waiting for an answer. "I'm not a boy," he went on.

"A man doesn't dare with no thought of danger," she pronounced. "That's a fool's work, or a boy's."

Tucked in bed, Ingledove passed an uneasy hour before she fell asleep; in the morning she woke to sunshine scattered in diamonds on the floor. Her canvas pack sagged on the braided rug Danagasta had made for her years ago. With a surge of feeling—anticipation? fear? excitement?—she recalled that they would be leaving in a few hours. She loved the rail station with its porters and ticket cage, the occasional dressed-up lady in heels and hat. It was long since she had been on a train, but she remembered the sashay of the coaches, the headlamp's blazing eye, and the whistle's singing out the crossings. When another train had come swooping past their own, she had heard a kind of heartbeat—the racketing sound as the train swept past, rising rhythmically and momentarily with each gap of air between the flying cars. In an hour or so they would be off, rocking across the Balsams toward the flooded villages of Hazel Creek.

And so that was how they had gone away from the house of safety—how Danagasta had sent them over the drowned lands to the back of beyond.

The Witchmaster's Sending

Danagasta had served as a sort of mother to the children since their own had died. It was a temporary arrangement at first. Mr. Townsend, who had employed their mother as a housekeeper before her illness, had taken on the responsibility of seeing that they were cared for and educated. In 1943 he had moved Lang, Ingledove, and the new housekeeper into his place in the city, and the young man who was his private secretary wrote many letters, trying to find the children's father. But the men were snatched up by the war and the need for experts versed in metallurgy. William, the secretary, became a soldier at eighteen; they had gotten two letters from him, then nothing. And even before the move, Mr. Townsend had traveled around the country, doing work for the government. He owned other homes, or so Danagasta claimed, and they were left to their own devices in the big house with its ranks of windows and mammoth fireplaces with copper surrounds and box-beam mantels. She called him the Copper Baron and was careful to dust his furniture and keep the windows sparkling, in case he should return unexpectedly.

During the war she had turned the backyard into a little farm with a cow and chickens and a kitchen garden, and they had managed well enough. The neighbors looked askance at the old woman in her long country skirts and aprons, but she kept the front lawn in good order and bothered no one. When a drive to collect scrap iron or paper was begun, no one scavenged more diligently than she.

"Can't have them barons in a frenzy with me," she would explain, winking at Ingledove.

Danagasta had simply appeared on the porch of Mr. Townsend's house in Hazel Creek. On the third day of Marm's illness, he had opened the door and found her there, eyes shut. Perhaps she was dozing or just resting. Part Cherokee and part Scottish, Danagasta had a strong, plain face the color of clay smoked in the fire. But when she opened her eyes, Mr. Townsend was startled and jumped a little, they were that dark and piercing. She might have been waiting a long time, there on the porch with her linen sack of clothes in one hand and a parcel of roots and leaves in the other. Or perhaps she had mysteriously appeared, like a sleight-of-hand trick.

"I'll tell you fer why," she answered the puzzled man. "To cook and clean and dose that sick servant womern in there." She talked in the way of the natives along Hazel Creek when she arrived, but as time passed she didn't always speak like them.

"I can talk some of the old Cherokee tongue from before the Removal," she explained to the children much later. "I can talk the mountain speech like these here miners and such. And I can talk English like in the furrin towns. That makes three languages. That's enough to satisfy," she added.

But no matter what mode of language she used, they were never able to find out how she had known their need or where she had come from. "That old witch," Doc Riter called her. When he cautioned her not to make "woods potions" for his feverish patient, she just folded her arms over flat breasts and frowned at him. Lang remembered Danagasta singing under her breath at their mother's bedside:

Little whirlwind, Adawehi,
Asleep in chestnut trees
At mountain's foot, Adawehi—
Rise up, rise up, small breeze,
To sweep this sickness far away,
To sweep this silt away.
Let killing grains forever stay
Banished from the day.

Arise, and scatter dust in play,
Adawehi, whirlwind,
Awaken to our mortal fray,
Protect us from the end
That comes too soon, with dust and fire:
The Adawehi's wind
Can heal the earth with mighty gyre
Of dance that makes and mends.

"No earthly use." The singer had rested a hand on the boy's shoulder. And when Marm died, Danagasta stayed.

"I didn't rightly know how to get rid of her," Mr. Townsend told his secretary; "but she's a good plain cook, and she works hard." So that was that.

When Ingledove pestered the housekeeper about why she'd come, she never answered the same way twice.

"Knew ill luck was featherin' into you'uns," she would say, sounding mountain-bred.

Or she might whisper something in Cherokee that made them go silent, because that always meant she wouldn't say another word. And why was it the Cherokee language from the time—or so she claimed—of the forced removal of the tribe to the West? The brother and sister got no answer to that one.

"The Masterest Witchmaster sent me," she muttered in Ingledove's ear one afternoon as the girl sat at her feet with a needle and coarse thread, stringing the beans called *leather britches*. In the winter they would boil them, pod and all. Her helper paused, needle in the air, and scrutinized Danagasta's face.

"What did you say?"

The old woman smiled slightly, with a knowing quirk of the lips, and told no more.

The children had lived in Asheville for some years now. Although they had a fierce loyalty to each other, they were not confidants as they might have been if nearer in age. But Marm had had two stillborn children between Lang and Ingledove, and they seemed separated not only by the years but by some gap left by the missing brother and sister they had never known.

Perhaps it was not that; perhaps it was only the bad fortune of spending their childhood in a place that was doomed to be swept away by the second of the World Wars. The War Department needed the power of the dam and, between the power company and the Tennessee Valley Authority, wiped the creeksides clean of all life to get it.

And yet there had been a time, a wonderful, almost mythical time, in which Hazel Creek had seemed the answer to a settler's fantasy of America. Arteries of copper branched through the slopes, some of the veins almost thirty feet wide, with metal so pure it could be molded in the hand. The Eagle Creek mine, where Ingledove and Lang's father worked for some years, was a great, upside-down money tree, its center trunk sunk more than two thousand feet into the ground and its boughs stretched to every side. Gold nuggets were the berries on those branches. Along the creek the land was sweet and arable, with plenty of water. It was a country big and rich enough for some legendary giant.

"If only nobody'd ever found us out," the boy would say, wistful for that lost world. He could tell stories about the northern lumber barons who came to rape the woods at the end of the last century with their great splash dams that, once opened, would roar and foam, juggling logs down the creek and into the Little Tennessee River and on to the lumber mills in Chattanooga. He said the old-timers boasted of walnut trees thirty feet in diameter, of immense cherries and cucumbers and chestnuts and buckeyes and poplars—a hundred kinds, all outsized and lordly. A single tree could supply the lumber for a house. When he was young, their grandfather had worked for a later outfit, the Ritter Lumber Company, sweeping and bagging the "doodling dust" left by the saws, and later as a pond man, washing the logs and steering them toward the mill with a long spiked pole. He'd known Horace Kephart, who wrote a book that made Hazel Creek famous for a time, though the old man always spat when he mentioned Kephart's name.

"Made us look allurs in a rippit," he complained, "or like a pack of dottle-headed shummicks camped in a backhouse."

Lang liked to repeat his grandpa's sayings, though Ingledove could never quite tell whether he was proud of their pithy vigor or else fascinated yet half-ashamed.

"I don't remember any of those stories," she told her brother.

"You were too young," he said.

But that life had passed like a dream: the copper mines, the farms now overtaken by scrub, and the loggers with crosscut saws. Their father, seeing the end of things ahead, had gone off to South America, looking for his fortune, and had never sent for them or come home again. Lang believed that their parents had been unhappy together long before the departure. He recalled Pappy reproaching his wife for leaving her heart in the far mountains, so that he had only half a woman—as if he had married a changeling instead of flesh and blood. "Don't raise such a ruction," she had whispered.

If their mother had not become cook and housekeeper to a rich copper man, the brother and sister would have been dependent on the community when she died. Doc Riter, the only doctor within thirty miles, had tried to save her. Both the children remembered him sitting up all night with their mother, dripping medicine between her parted lips and changing the compress on her forehead. She died the next morning, just after daybreak, and Doc waded through wet grass and scrub, picking a bouquet of wildflowers to lay across her folded arms. "Your mother was a unique woman. She had a gentle, beauty-loving soul," he told the children.

Not long afterward, the copper man carried them from Hazel Creek to his fine home in Asheville with its big arched door and black-and-white tiles in the front hall, above which climbed a wide staircase to the square promenade on the second floor. They lived in some upstairs rooms with Danagasta, for Mr. Townsend had stayed away throughout the war, and afterward he went straight to his holdings in Colorado. The housekeeper ran the place, carried out his infrequent orders, and made sure Lang and Ingledove were clothed and fed.

She simply shrugged when they asked if he would ever return.

"What that man does, who can say?" she added, lighting her pipe and shutting her eyes to signal that the subject was closed.

THE DROWNED LANDS

Ingledove let her hand trail in the water beside the rowboat and by moonlight saw the minnows rise to kiss her fingers.

"I hate them," Lang whispered, his voice hoarse.

"Who do you hate?" she murmured, already knowing.

"The TVA and the government and Alcoa. I hate them for buying up and ruining these towns, Almond and Forney and Japan and the rest. I hate them for driving our father away and killing our mother. And I hate them for digging up our dead and not letting them rest in peace. We would still be living in our own house with our own family if none of this had happened."

But it did, Lang, it did, she thought. And their mother hadn't been killed, not exactly—it was just that a chain of events had forced her from home, and she had died afterward, a servant in another man's house. The fault had been money, or the lack of it. There was no use in talking to her brother.

Barely seventeen, he considered himself a man and far older than she—more than mere years could count. Yet she could keep what she thought to herself, and he could not.

In the night the reservoir had a kind of fairy glamour, and it was easy to forget the raw red clay banks that loomed above the waterline. The stars and the clouds were mirrored on its surface just as finely as if it were a real body of water and not a false dead thing made by men.

"We're sliding over a townsite right now," Lang said, then laughed in a way that made Ingledove jerk up her head and stare. Both of them had been passionate children, but he had not learned to curb his feelings.

When she looked back, the minnows had fled. Her fingers were ruffling the surface of the water, tumbling a reflected cloud.

"I like to think that, down there, the people are still going in and out of the houses." She could picture them, drifting like ghosts from the doors, pale in the green murk. The spirit children's voices wavered up as bubbles, shattering against the ceiling of air.

But it wasn't so. Not even the dead remained, for more than a thousand had been tugged from their graves and reburied on higher ground. Even their own mother had been yanked from the earth and planted again, and Ingledove could never forget the protesting screech of the nails in the wood as the men pried the coffin from the mud. The slots of abandoned graves lay open to the water, and who knew what creatures had come to lurk there?

She shook her head, as if to drive away the morbid thought. It was lovely here on the lake, with the moon shining on the white trail made by the oars. The water wriggled, as though containing some magic vigor and being more than the still, trapped liquid behind a dam.

"The moon's almost full," she said; "only two or three more days left."

Lang leaned into the rowing, the blades sweeping them farther and farther into the world where they had once lived, the lost towns and hamlets of Hazel Creek. "The back of beyond" people were already calling what remained, because it was so hard to reach. Their mother would have warmed to the fresh mystery of the district. Marm had populated their childhood with magical animals and spirits whose whimsical kindness could be as treacherous as their "dev'lin."

"There aren't any houses, you know," Lang said. Ingledove supposed he was still thinking about the village under the water. "Don't you remember? A team of men tore up the best ones. Chestnut boards, three inches thick and almost two feet wide, came out of a house down the street. Then they cut down the trees and chopped the rhododendron and scrub. Like scraping off a beard. It was ugly, ugly."

He lifted the oars and rested. The rowboat slowed, gliding in the moonlight. They had found where it had been hidden, just as promised, and to their surprise the craft, which looked worn and old, had proved tight. It must once have been some sensible color but had faded to a forget-me-not blue, and no tinge of gloss remained.

"I know," Ingledove said. She lifted her hand from the water and let the drops fall back. A minnow rushed forward, as if he thought a splash might mean something to eat. Searching in her pocket, she sprinkled a few crumbs over the gunwale.

"What I'd never forget," she added, "is standing on the grave-yard hill at Possum Hollow and watching fires."

"You mean when the TVA men burned the Franklin store and the warehouse. I was there, too." Lang flexed his arms, then took up the oars.

"I remember the roar and crackle of the fire and the sparks shooting up as if from a wizard's wand. And there were little green flames darting like jeweled snakes along the copper."

"Someday they'll be sorry that they didn't save those old villages for the national park," he said. "People in cities hardly even know where wood comes from—don't even imagine such a thing as a logging or mining town." He laughed again. "You know, I hate them most for making us learn to talk good English and think thoughts like that—we would've stayed here all our lives and never known that we were old-fashioned and strange, living in another world. We would have been content with Marm and Pappy and never known to call them *Mother* and *Father*. It would've been better that way."

His sister didn't argue, though she thought that Lang fit in quite well back in Asheville. The other boys liked him because he was bold in manner and agile at games. The teachers liked him because he worked furiously, though they didn't know, as his sister did, that it was in part because he thought he could drive himself into a different life—what sort, he didn't know, except that he would be a wealthy man. There was no going back to a former existence, because that had been swept away by the first water pounding into the reservoir, the churned-up clay staining the gush to the red of dried blood. Oh, they all admired him—the inhabitants of their second life. Like her, he was fair-haired with hazel eyes, but he was the more handsome. Both were startling in appearance, dark and light together, but he already had a man's body, muscular and small-waisted, and girls were drawn to him. Ingledove was not yet pretty, for she seemed not quite finished. She was slender, starting to bud, though no more than that; people often said she had lovely eyes or hair or lips, as if they could see only a piece of her at a time.

"Like snakes." Lang repeated her words, and she was sorry that she'd spoken. He must be thinking about the nightmare he'd had the night before they left, and how Danagasta had been upset by what she called "the ghost snake" from his dream.

He was silent, and the landscape seemed asleep except for the splash of the oars. It was such a long way over the water! He had lingered by the faded periwinkle shell of the rowboat and looked across the glistening lake, but he'd made no complaint. When Ingledove had said that it seemed too far to row, he shrugged and replied, "Why shouldn't it take hard work to go from one world to another?" A cloud slipped over the moon, and she began to nod. Often when she lay down at night, she heard a kind of babbling, as if people were talking a room away, and as she yielded to dream, she could hear voices. Now only half-awake, she wondered whether the former inhabitants were chatting of old times in the deep well of the reservoir.

"What was that?" Lang's voice jerked her to consciousness.

She looked around, made uneasy by the immense expanse of water. More than ten thousand acres, Danagasta had told her. At once she felt alert, remembering that at the bottom were remains of houses, stone foundations beneath the rooms, things that could not be salvaged or burned but that had been chained to the earth, and fish that swam through cellars and attics.

"What was it? What did you hear?"

The rowboat spun slowly on the lake as he held still, listening. Around them stretched the miles of liquid moonlight.

"I don't know," he said at last; "maybe it was the sound of a woman's voice. Singing, or crying out. Over there." He nodded toward their destination. "And for a minute I thought there was a white figure—see that dazzle on the water? I could have sworn a girl was walking on the surface there. But that couldn't be so."

"Maybe you fell asleep, like me. Or maybe you had too much moonshine in your eyes." Ingledove smiled at him, making light of his unease to calm her own. "Who knows? Someone from Hazel Creek might be ahead of us, traveling to pay respects to their families buried in Bone Valley or Cable Branch or Laney or some other cemetery. Or maybe it's one of the Little People from Mother's and Danagasta's stories. Remember Marm saying that the spirit lands were only a skip away? I'd love to see a fairy skimming over the water." She glanced up; the wind had blown the clouds aside. "Look at the stars, Lang. Marm loved to sit in the yard at dusk and watch the sky. One time I asked her where stars came from, and she told me, 'Hit's fool's gold that's got busted to flanders in a pounding mill. Hit's a power of shine.' She looked happy when she said it. I don't know why some words lodge, when there's so much I can't and want to recall. But I remember that."

"Yes," he said, "she loved the stars more than anybody I've met since. There was a power of shine in her, too, I guess." But he looked about them and listened a while longer before reaching for the oars and setting his back to the far shore.

THE BURNING WATERS

"The hills are turning blue." Lang stood and surveyed the slope of stones. "We need to go back to the camp before it gets dark, or we'll never find the way."

Ingledove's fingertips grazed the stone. She wasn't listening to him. After saying a prayer for each of the dead, she had trimmed the grass of their graves with scissors, clipping around the worn lamb headstones and the newer marker of their mother. Never set properly, the heavy slab had leaned and sunk into the earth and was already hard to read, the words obscured by rain and soil.

"Look at this." She tugged at the roots of grass, tearing at the matted stems. "There's something more I didn't see here . . ."

The letters were cut in a different style from the rest, as if they had been added later. *A daughter of Adantis.* Slowly she repeated the words.

"What does it mean?"

Lang shook his head, squatting to take a closer look. "I've heard of that—a place, I'd guess."

"You know, I think that was the name of a country in Marm's make-believe stories, the ones she would tell after the lights were out and I was half asleep. They seemed more real than anything else, then—I felt so sure that her creatures were roaming nearby, in the shadows under the mountains. *Adantis.* I wonder who chose those words?"

"I guess it was Mr. Townsend."

"Maybe it was Danagasta."

"Maybe. And I remember the name, too, but I can't tell from where. It just sounds familiar. I don't remember it being in Marm's stories, though a lot of them stick in my mind."

Ingledove cleaned the scissors of dirt, wiping them across the grass.

"But I do," she said stubbornly. "I'm sure it was in some of them—the fairy tale sort, I believe."

He turned away from the sight of his sister, kneeling among the graves. "I always liked the ones about heroes rushing off on quests for the Laidly Worm or some such thing. But my favorites were about her ancestors in Scotland, fighting under the border warlords. They were wild reivers who plundered their neighbors. I liked it when she told about the Cherokee, slipping through the shadows of trees. And settlers as small as bugs against the wild mountains, finding some hollow they liked and making shelters of sticks and mud to keep off the rains. Anyway, let's go."

He started up the slope, stopping once to make sure she

was following. From the top they could see the far glimmering of the reservoir.

"It was the stories about magic lands and sorcery that I liked best," she said softly, but her brother did not hear. He looked foreign, dressed in the clothes that the housekeeper had hidden in their rucksacks—without so much as a word about it! There were long-sleeved linen shirts for Lang, belted with a woven sash, and close-fitting leather pants that reminded them vaguely of Indian leggings. For Ingledove, Danagasta had packed handwoven gowns, cut low, with narrow waists, and there were sashes like the ones that belted the men's shirts. Hemmed about four inches above the ankle, the skirts belled out for easy walking. Why had she done it? For that matter, where had she gotten the weaver's cloth and sashes? The girl imagined that these were a style of dress Danagasta's great-grandparents might have worn.

"What's this?" Lang had tugged out a shirt, then turned his pack upside down and spilled the clothes across the grass.

"That Danagasta! What's she up to now?" He hadn't been angry; instead, he had laughed, springing from his knees and unbuttoning his shirt so that Ingledove caught a flash of muscled chest. She turned her head away, and when she looked again he had changed: the leather pants and loose shirt with its green sash making him seem displaced in time.

In high spirits, he had gone to survey himself in the lake's waters.

"Check what's in yours," he called back to her, and she obeyed.

When newly attired, she had felt unsettled, gazing at a reflection of what seemed two strangers. The metamorphosis had seemed to prophesy further transformation to come. It had declared a transit from the ordinary world, even more plainly than the crossing had done.

"See there?" Lang pointed to a glimpse of reservoir. The graceful linen sleeve, cut full and hanging in folds, caught Ingledove's eye. "There was a long sandbar just about where that patch of water is shining, and the pastor used to lead the people there to be baptized. Sometimes they'd go singing, with flowers in their arms. The ones to be baptized would be wearing nothing but long white chrisoms. The Baptist preacher would make them crash down like a plank. Then he'd haul them up again."

The girl nodded. She didn't remember. "Look there at the sunset. It's making the water pink."

He paused, following her gaze, before turning from the graveyard. A few structures near the creek had been saved deliberately, kept for the national park that was to preserve what was left of the mountains from the rich barons of these and later days. Lang had insisted that they avoid the sites, cautious of meeting anyone who might order him home to Danagasta. They had hunted for and found a snug place to camp in the woods—a tiny cabin made of adzed logs, with still-unbroken panes on each side of the door and frieze windows under the eaves. The builder's children or grandchildren had added a paneled door in front of the original plank one from years before and had built narrow stone shafts at each end to replace what must have been wood chimneys.

On first arrival, the brother and sister had heaped leaves and ferns to make a soft bed. Probably it was as good a mattress as the settlers had slept on.

"We should've left earlier," the boy said aloud. "No matter, since we're so close." He strode more quickly, half running on the downhill slope. "Come on," he called, not looking back.

She hurried to catch him. It would be cold in the mountains at night—coals and dry wood awaited their return to the cabin.

The bones of a dead hickory on the crest above were streaked with an intense rose.

"There was a farm here," Lang said, panting. "Sort of a sawed-off place hanging on to the hillside, with apple trees."

Ingledove didn't speak because of the pain in her side as she followed close behind him on the upward path. She was glad when he halted under the dead claws of the tree and stared back at the reservoir, now a reflective sheet of fire. She bent over, setting her hands on her knees, a coppery saliva in her mouth, noticing that the bare limbs cast long crooked shadows on the scrub laurel and saplings.

"Listen! There's that sound I heard, out on the water . . ." He stood still, his breath slowing.

Ingledove could hear it now, a distant wordless billowing of song that must be a female voice. As if someone were calling to the coming night and the smoldering lake, the girl thought, shivering from the coolness of the air and a hint of the uncanny in the notes.

"Lang!" She didn't like the way he had sealed her out, closing his eyes to the sunset and the path, caught by the sorcery of the song.

He didn't respond. His features were as motionless and alien as a mask. The outrush of melody seemed to bleed into the burning western sky.

"We've got to go," she said, shaking her brother's arm.

"What?" He looked at her, a faint hint of annoyance passing across his face. The singing began to die away, almost as if it had needed the nourishment of their attention and was bereft without it.

"Let's go. You looked peculiar, Lang." She could no longer see deep into the forest. But the voice was gone now, wasn't it? She could almost hear it; perhaps she did, or else the echo of the sound was still pressing on her thoughts.

He shrugged and, crossing the shadow of the tree, dived into the path below.

"It's not far now," he said when she caught up. "I was just thinking about something. We've done what we came for, and it's only the second day. We could go traipsing for a bit. Maybe walk to Cades Cove. I rode there one time with Marm on horseback. It was a long outing, but pretty. I don't know why we went, unless it was to sell some of Marm's sourwood honey. And there was something strange . . ."

"Well?"

"We met an old man with a big walking stick in the forest. I'd forgotten all about him," Lang added. "He gave Marm a bunch of yellow flowers and a piece of polished rock. I used to see glimmers of faces in it. That's what I thought, anyway. Marm let me play with it like a toy."

"What happened to it? I don't remember anything like that."

"It got lost. Marm thought the thing was stolen. Who knows—maybe I dropped the stone in the well. She ransacked the house and yard." Lang brushed a cobweb from his face. "So how about it? We could go deeper into the mountains and just wander. Wouldn't that be fun?"

His sister's instinct was to say "No!" But she wanted to be with him and please him. Before she could answer, he threw out an arm to point.

"Look—there's the cabin."

The two raced the rest of the way and jumped over the doorway just as night swooped on the hollow and covered it entirely. Panting, Ingledove sprawled on the floor while Lang felt in the darkness for matches and lit Danagasta's candle lantern. The light looked like water—a wavering brightness lapping at the dark. She stared about uneasily, remembering the ghosts under the lake.

"If you start the fire, I'll get out some food," he suggested. He didn't seem bothered by the gloom.

After raking the ash from the morning's coals, she set a nest of dry weeds and slivers of wood on top. The tinder ignited as she blew gently on the coals. Ingledove added sticks and downed limbs they had gathered before breakfast. The crackling promise of warmth to come made her relax a little, and she sat back on her heels. Still, she kept expecting a voice to break out from a corner of the cabin, and it wasn't until fire bloomed on the hearth that she let go of her nervousness.

So in the end she forgot to answer Lang's question, and later when she remembered, it seemed too late to deny him. It wasn't as though she didn't want an adventure. She had dreamed of Hazel Creek and of wandering through the mountains many times in her room in the Copper Baron's house, safe between the four posts of the bed.

THE BILLOWING SONG

On the third day since their departure from the cabin, Ingledove no longer had any idea where they were, though her brother frequently consulted a compass and a topographical map of the mountains. Their supplies of cornmeal and dried meat had been augmented by berries and fruit from an abandoned orchard near the reservoir. Lang was unexpectedly cheerful, even when they had hiked out of range of the beautiful voice and passed two days without hearing a single note. His sister sometimes suspected that he was searching for the mysterious singer.

The mountains grew steeper, with fewer trails, and in the evenings the two sank to sleep as soon as they crawled into their bedrolls under a roof of oiled canvas, tied between two trees. By the fourth morning, Ingledove felt sure that she could never find her way home without Lang.

That night, Ingledove woke to see Lang perched on a pack

outside their makeshift tent, his face lifted to the moon that hovered above the ridgeline. She could hear a drop of dew spatter on the canvas fly. He was leaning forward, his face bathed in light. The girl sat up and called his name softly, but he didn't hear—and in a minute she realized why. He was listening to the voice again. A shrunken outcry, the sound came from a distance. She rubbed her arms, glad for the quick flare of warmth under her hands. She didn't like that song. It made her uneasy; its outpouring reminded her of the clouds that streamed from mist-piled gulfs between the mountains.

Could something be calling them? Certainly *she* had no desire to answer. Alluring Lang, perhaps? His body was pressed forward, trembling with the chill of the mountain night and perhaps with anticipation. In the morning she didn't mention what she had seen.

While he was taking notes in a pocket journal, consulting the compass that Mr. Townsend had sent him from Denver, she asked when they would be turning back.

"You don't want to go yet, do you?" He spoke absently, as if his thoughts were not on her and not even on the elegant compass that swiveled neatly into a steel case engraved with his name.

"I just thought . . ." She looked across the valley. They had been moving higher for several days, and the blue hills lapped endlessly away. Wisps were detaching from a mass of clouds socked into the depths between mountains. Tall stems of yellow flowers lashed and held by the pale orange of the parasitical love vine glowed in the morning light. "I wish Marm were here with us, to see it all."

Jotting in his notebook, Lang took no notice.

He wants to go on, Ingledove reflected. *And I—I am afraid of the big spaces between the near mountains and the blue distances behind them that are overlapping ridges but look like some otherworldly place, a country from the moon. It's like a land far away and long ago, where mysteries might wander, lovely storybook ladies or dragons and other creatures nobody has ever seen. He's not afraid; he wants to explore those ghostly regions. And if I don't belong with him, where do I fit?*

"Ready?" His voice was quiet, and when she looked he was smiling at her. She felt a rush of tenderness for him, older than she and bound to leave her soon, perhaps to vanish into some foreign country, as their father had done, or to fight in some new war yet to be born and named. This might be their last chance to be together, because in the spring he would be finished with school. And so she hoisted the pack into place and smiled at him in return.

The mornings were splendid, sun igniting the clouds to dazzling white. They followed old ruts that Lang surmised must have been beaten by the Cherokee and early settlers. Ingledove liked the rolling paths but grew to dread the steep sections half washed away by spring torrents, where she had to cling to trunks of trees and rhododendron and sometimes call for help from her brother. By early afternoon they would be tired, often napping for an hour on warm boulders in the sun, once ousting a red fox from his siesta. On waking, they continued until the first long shadows of dusk began to slip from coves and nooks. Then they stopped and tied up the canvas roof and spread their bedding beneath, afterward cooking a circle of johnnycake to eat with strips of dried meat or berries picked in the afternoon.

The rhythmic pattern continued with little variation. One night they camped under a ledge of rock and watched a storm blow in from the west; a jag of lightning struck close enough to make their hair stand on end. The next morning the split trunk of an oak still smoked in the early coolness. Once they saw a family of bears out harvesting fruit, their big paws raking at the berries. The girl glimpsed a tiny bird harry a raven across a valley. Occasionally they spotted small animals running or a herd of deer standing impossibly still in dappled shade. Mostly it was an intricate pattern of green with flowers that they had known as small children but whose names they could not summon and trails crossed by trickling rivulets where salamanders crept over the stones.

Ingledove lost count of the days and the direction toward Asheville, though her brother still wrote in his little book and hauled out the compass whenever they paused to rest. They washed their clothes in icy pools and spread them on the rocks. Soon it seemed like an existence that could go on forever.

So it was a shock when they stumbled on a house.

Perhaps the cabin didn't deserve the title of *house*, being worn and ramshackle, but it had three rooms and peaked rafters and a stick chimney. The roof was covered with clumps of moss, among which grew an occasional shrub or flower.

Lang glanced at the sky, where clouds were burgeoning, bruised to indigo.

"What do you think?"

It wasn't like him to ask. But she was not displeased by this appeal. "If nobody lives there, why not go in? Or if they do and seem friendly enough, we could pay to spend the night. Maybe we could buy some cornmeal and tea. There's smoke . . ."

Approaching the cabin, they saw a figure bent over a pot with a child clutching her skirts.

"Hello," Lang called.

A woman whirled to face them, her hand going to a string at her neck.

"I didn't mean to frighten you," he added, smiling a little at her astonished face. Or maybe it was at her ugliness, Ingledove thought—it had startled them both. She had a coarse brown mustache that gave her an oddly rakish look. The face was wary and weather-beaten, with an uptilted nose and full, ruddy cheeks, and the body was as stout as a wringer washer, with skirts cinched high under her breasts. Ingledove was surprised to see that the clothes she wore resembled her own, though there was a handkerchief tucked in the low-cut bodice. She noticed that what the woman had touched at her throat was a cross made of silver, and that the child wore an identical one strung around his neck.

"*You* can't scare me," the woman replied, a tinge of disdain in her manner.

"Lang," Ingledove whispered, seeing that the reddened fingers were curved around a knife.

He nodded slightly. He had seen it, too.

She slipped the blade into a sleeve and went back to pounding at the laundry with a thick wooden pestle. The child peered out of her skirts at them, and Ingledove was surprised to see nothing of the mother's redness of skin—the little one was pale, with slight features and high forehead.

She began dipping out her laundry and spreading the garments on some rhododendron close by.

"It's about to rain," Ingledove offered.

"Won't hurt clothes," she said briefly, scowling at them through a veil of steam.

"We thought maybe we could stay the night," Lang said; "we would pay you."

She paused in her stooping, cocking her head and giving him a look from the corner of her eye.

"I want to go," Ingledove whispered. "I don't like it here."

Releasing the battling stick, the washerwoman came forward. Drops of water stood up on her mustache and beaded her hair.

"Let's see the money," she ordered.

"Let's see the rooms, then," Lang said, half joking, giving his sister's hand a squeeze.

The interior was dark but appeared clean enough. There were two beds in a back lean-to and another in the main room.

"Clean sheets on the one by the fireplace." Missing teeth made the smile resemble the leer of a madwoman. A single spike ruled the lower jaw in lonely splendor.

"What's your name?" Ingledove asked the child, who had not yet let go of his mother's skirts.

"His name's Ild," she snapped. "Will it do? Let's see your money." She headed back outside, to where "the light's good."

She took what was offered and turned it in her fingers, holding the green presidential face up to the sun. "I never liked foreign stuff," she muttered to herself. "But some do, some do. And paper's just flimsy. I like Adantan coin. But I'll take it," she decided.

"Adantan coin?" the girl asked.

"Who don't like it best?" The newly created landlady stuffed the now-folded bill inside her dress.

"Our marm was a daughter of Adantis," Ingledove said hesitantly.

"Of course she was." She scrutinized the girl, her forehead puckering with concentration. "Soft in the head?" she asked Lang.

He flashed her a smile. "Well, a little," he agreed. "But my sister does very well just the same."

"There's melon-headed shummicks in Adantis, just the same as in the lands beyond. That's for certain." She nodded at the silent Ild, as though she wanted him to remember her words.

"Well, she's no shummick," the young man said, "though she may be a bit melon-headed."

Ingledove stepped hard on his foot.

"Ow! Bad girl!" He laughed heartily, so that the woman gave him a probing look.

"Madam, I am no shummick," his sister said slowly, mustering all her dignity but only making Lang laugh the harder. "You misconceive and malign me in thinking so."

"Poor little melon. Listen to her talk."

"Yes, ma'am." The young man shook his head in mock sadness.

After the mother had trudged off to the washpot with her son still half-hidden in her skirts, Ingledove pinched Lang.

"Ouch!" Rubbing his arm, he looked at her, not at all abashed.

"You let her think I was a *melon!*"

"I thought it was funny," he said, picking up their packs. "Besides, who's the melon? Mistress One-Fang didn't even understand what you meant when you got so grand and hoity-toity."

"Listen," she said, bounding beside him as he carried their burdens into the house; "that's just ignorance. It doesn't matter so much when it comes to spending the night. But I really don't like it here. That Ild is a queer little newt, afraid of everything. And she's odd—we don't even know who she is."

"She doesn't know who we are, either." The boy dipped his head to go through the open door.

"That's right—she never asked. Curious."

Setting the rucksacks at the foot of a bedstead, Lang pulled off the coverlet and examined the sheets, running a hand over the bedding.

"It's clean. Boiled handwoven linen by the look of it. Even the Copper Baron doesn't have real linen, hey? Besides, it's going to be an awfully dirty night, judging by the clouds. There's nothing to worry about."

"Maybe not," she admitted, feeling as anxious as before. "Maybe it's nothing. But what about 'daughter of Adantis'? What does it mean?"

Lang was kneeling on the hearth, peering into the chimney. "Thought I saw something odd sticking out. There are some worn-out children's shoes fastened to the sides. To kick out witches, I guess." He glanced at his sister. "Adantis again—

you're right; it is peculiar. Probably some mountain freema-
sonry that we were too young to know in Hazel Creek."

"Maybe so."

"Go see if I left anything in the grass, will you? I unfastened
my pack to get out the money, and now I don't see my knife.
I'll start a fire and get going on supper."

Ingledove paused at the door, watching the woman hoist
another garment with the stick. The strange little boy had
buried his face in her skirts. She must not be so bad if he loved
her that much, the girl reflected. The weather was ghastlier
than before, with a wind flipping over the leaves to show their
pale undersides while turbulent clouds mounted to the very
rooftree of the sky. But on the ground it was strangely bright,
the color of the foliage seemingly lit from within.

She saw the mother peer at the far corner of the clearing
and then grope for her necklace. Someone was crossing the
corner of the yard, dressed in a white gown that shone in
the greenish sunlight that promised a storm to come. This
stranger was everything their hostess was not: slim and fair,
with a narrow waist. Before vanishing into elderberry shrubs,
she swung around and gazed straight at the cabin and at Ingledove in the doorway.

The large eyes were set slightly too far apart; she had a small
straight nose and a mouth that was prettily curved, though the
lips were rather narrow. Not flawless, she nonetheless conveyed the air of a great beauty, with her pale unblemished skin
and the long shining coils of hair. Ingledove guessed that she
might be in her mid-thirties, although there was an agelessness
about the face that made the years hard to measure.

The girl stood staring at the trembling twigs of the elderberries until they stilled. Then she remembered her errand and scurried over to the spot where the packs had lain. Sure enough, there was the knife glinting under some ginger leaves. She pocketed it, feeling the stares of the two onlookers.

"My brother lost something," she explained, lifting one hand to wave. They didn't respond, so she walked slowly toward them.

"What should we call you?" she asked.

The mother spat amber into the bushes, barely missing the white hem of a nightgown. Ild made a growling noise in his throat. He had taken the cross into his mouth and was now sucking on the silver like a pony with a bit.

"He don't like tobacco," she explained, sending another squirt into the grass. "You won't have need for my name, I reckon. But you can holler *Sally* if you have a mind to." She lifted a wide dripping skirt from the pot and slopped it onto a broken-down piece of fence.

"And who was that—the lady who came through the yard and looked at me?"

At this, Sally turned away and fished about in the kettle, hauling up a stained linen shift. Ild managed to wriggle between the pot and his mother—if she *was* his mother—until she knocked him aside with the stick. He didn't reproach her for that violence but climbed back onto his feet and took hold of her skirts.

It occurred to Ingledove that he never smiled. Although he seemed of an age to talk, he was completely wordless.

"I asked who the lady was . . ."

The boy bared his teeth, and she slowly retreated.

Inside, Lang was stretched out by the fire, tending a hoe-cake. Not for the first time, his sister thought how handsome he looked in Danagasta's linen shirts and leather. She sat on the floor beside him, feeling more disturbed than ever.

"What's up with the little melonhead?" His voice was lazy, and he yawned as he prodded the flat cake in the pan.

"Nothing, I guess. Here's your knife." Slipping it into his hand, she pressed his fingers. There wasn't any point in repeating her fears or in telling about the lady in white. She didn't want her brother to take a step from the room. If she hung a quilt from the iron rails of the bed, she could creep behind it to wash and change into nightclothes. They would sleep by the fire this night, and in the morning she would take the lead and traipse as fast as she could until they were far away from this place.

After supper they took to the bed, Ingledove fanning the pages of a book she had borrowed from school and Lang jotting down notes by candlelight. But she felt more and more apprehensive. Though the door to the cabin was propped wide to the rain, the atmosphere inside was sultry and humid. Ild was sitting in his mother's lap devouring a bowl of porridge, and Ingledove felt half-relieved to find out that he was truly human and capable of eating. Now and then his eyes would drift to her face, groping and intrusive like the fingers of the blind.

Then a shaft of lightning struck a boulder in the clearing, erupting from the rock like a fountain. For an instant afterward it was utterly silent, as if all sound had been sucked from the room. A candle guttered and went out. "Ah. I like a good storm when I'm comfortable and under a roof." Lang sighed and stretched out on the bed.

Ingledove remained upright, but she reached over and took his hand, which relaxed in her own. She kept staring at the rectangle of pouring rain that was the doorway. The outer world kept flashing on and off, illuminating momentarily a tangle of boughs caught in continual seizure. Closing her eyelids, she trembled, feeling the wind tearing up the valleys, ripping the leaves from the trees and juggling them high in the air, never letting one drop.

Opening her eyes as another shaft splintered against the ground near the cabin, she gasped. The lady in white was standing between the threshold and their bed. This time she was soaked, the gown clinging to every curve of her sinuous body, her features glazed by rain. Ingledove could hear the boy Ild jump from his mother's lap. Sally called to him in a low, urgent tone, but he did not respond. The uncanny part of the apparition was not the drenched clothing, nor the faint and enigmatic smile on the lovely face. The girl saw that she had been wrong, unless there were two dressed in identical white dresses or unless the figure had somehow changed in aspect: this was no woman in her thirties but someone of Lang's age. She glanced once at her brother and saw that he was leaning on one elbow, staring at the refugee from the storm.

Another bolt of lightning frizzled against stone, and Ingledove let out a cry of terror when a gust blew out the candles on the table as Sally leaned forward in her chair, calling to the child. Lang relit their own, but by then the visitor had vanished, and only a puddle of water on the floor marked where she had stood.

WILDINGS

Ingledove stayed awake until dim light showed at the open door. Then, finally, she let go. She slept hard and didn't wake until the sun had clambered over the clouds, halfway to the peak of sky.

When she slid out of bed, no one was left in the cabin, so she hurriedly peeled off her nightgown and dressed by the hearth, where the coals from breakfast were still red. Grabbing what was left of a johnnycake, she ventured out. The wind felt raw and fresh, scrubbing her cheeks with cold. Lang was nowhere in sight. Elderberries and laurel sprinkled her with chill drops as she paced the edge of the clearing.

On the far side of the house, she glimpsed Sally with Ild once again fastened to her skirts like a malnourished parasite. She stood watching, fascinated by the heavyset woman with her slip of a boy in tow. Sally was shoving her arms into the bushes, grabbing her soaked clothes and wringing them, spreading them to dry. Some heavy gowns had tangled in branches or wadded in heaps at the foot of laurel scrub. Though surely far too old for such behavior, Ild was sucking his thumb. The maternal arm flew out and clapped him across the ear. He made no remonstrance but slowly pulled the thumb from his mouth and stealthily drew his hand across his narrow chest and hid it in a pocket. His eyes were shining, but he didn't cry. Staring at the girl, he appeared absolutely impassive. Yet somehow he seemed to signal to his mother without speaking, for after the two had exchanged a look, she craned her head and gave the spectator one fierce glance.

Light-headed from lack of sleep, Ingledove drifted forward, the earth rolling and insubstantial to her feet.

"Why did you wash when it was bound to rain?" It wasn't what she meant to ask; it was as though her tiredness had uncorked her mouth and poured out the wrong words entirely.

"Onliest way to bring on water." Sally spoke curtly.

Ingledove wondered if she really thought that hanging up laundry would make it rain. Who could tell?

"Your daughter . . ."

The mountain woman spat and shook her head. She wasn't going to talk about the daughter. Ingledove tried again.

"Have you seen my brother?"

"Brother? No."

The girl felt too weary to be alarmed. Nor was she bothered by the brusque manner. To her surprise she felt the tug of a thread of pity as she observed the chapped hands wring the long twisted snakes of fabric. Lang could not be far, surely, and soon they would leave this spot and never return. But

Sally would go on living in the three-room cabin with the child . . .

Ild relaxed his hold on the gown and gave her a smile. It was sweet, as welcome as a sparkle of sun after a long tempest.

"You're as shy as a fawn," she told him.

"Shy as a woodscolt," his mother added scornfully. The little boy gave her a level look in which could be discerned no affection. "A poor measly outsider," she went on, thrusting him away.

Was he, then, not Sally's own son? Perhaps he was a foster child. Feeling in her pocket, Ingledove drew out a knotted cord and began playing cat's cradle, her fingers flicking easily at the string. He drew near to watch.

"There! I call this one *the castle*. See the doorway and the four towers?"

Collapsing the edifice into a cradle and then into a tangle, she sighed, her thoughts shifting to Lang and his disappearance, the ghostly figure in the night, her own wish to flee the cabin. She would have to ask again about the young woman, but there seemed a constraint on her words—as if she could not ask what she most wanted to know. Or perhaps she was afraid of the answer.

"More," the boy demanded.

"Done," Sally told him, slapping a wet shift onto a lichened fence post. "Done. Leave her be. It's gone all catawampus now."

"What?" Ingledove almost touched the dark helmet of hair with her fingertips, but some uncertain expresson in the wide eyes halted her. "More cat's cradle, you mean? Maybe later. Before I go. I promise."

The modeling of the delicate face seemed to alter subtly, the nostrils faintly flaring, the chin becoming more set and stubborn.

"Ild," his mother warned.

Growling, he ran at the girl and nipped her arm near the wrist.

"Oh!" Her startled exclamation was as shrill and sudden as a bird's cry.

"Low-down little wilding!" Sally backhanded her son, knocking him to the moss. Her face was as tense and angry as his own, but there was something else there that a stranger could not quite read. Was she frightened? And of whom? Ild, it seemed . . . What mother feared her own child?

"Show it," Sally ordered. She studied the teethmarks for a long time before she judged them to be "safe." "No need for a poultice," she muttered.

Ingledove took a few steps back. Absurdly, the playground question and answer "Mother, may I?" and "Yes, you may" came into her head. No politeness here, no usual give-and-take between parent and child: what a wretched corner this was!

Ild crouched on a patch of moss stars, his knees muddy, eyes on Sally's face, a single tear adrift on one cheek. There was an earnestness and even an unchildlike anguish in his expression that made his mother gasp. In an instant he sprang at her with a howl, leaping onto her bosom so that she staggered and caught at his shirt, holding him at arm's length. Yet he struggled and strained toward her, whining like a hurt dog, until she let go and he was propelled into her embrace.

Letting out a single note of alarm, Ingledove stood trembling, sure that the boy meant to bite at Sally—his face, stricken by some desperate need, seemed wholly alien.

"Mine," he sobbed, "mine." He lunged upward, grasping in a frantic embrace, his hands gripping Sally's shoulders, head butting against her breasts until she gave in wholly and knelt on the soaked moss with her arms around the child. Wrenching cries racked his frame, and he continued to call out "Mine! Mine! Mine!" in his passion.

"Hush, hush," Sally murmured. "You be a biddable young'un, Ild. Hush."

They had forgotten about Ingledove, who could not stop herself from witnessing the scene, her legs still weak from fright. In her sleepless state the sight of the two seemed like a dream, something part joy and part nightmare.

"Tell me," the child insisted, the words broken by a hiccup.

"Mine, and not a woodscolt," she promised. "Ild but not ill-begotten. And not wild but mine, forever and ever." But her voice seemed to have an edge of dread and doubt, though she bent and stared him in the eyes without blinking.

"My blossom," the boy whispered, his fingers straying over her face.

His *blossom*! Ingledove couldn't conceive of anything more incongruous than this mountaineer with her bristling mustache being called a flower. She remembered the yellow petals trapped inside the skeins of love vine—perhaps if she could see that linkage aright, its strings would be a cat's-cradle castle sheltering blooming princesses. Perhaps from the right angle of vision the woman was beautiful and understandable, but she could not see it.

Sally pressed her lips against the boy's forehead, and he arched upward, kissing her on the mouth. And so she loved him, it seemed, and he her in return. If that love were a flower, it would not be a stainless lily of the field but a thorny castellated thistle: a spike with sharp flanges and buds that exploded into deep purple silks powdered with gold. Ingledove had seen such prickly weeds in Danagasta's garden, rearing in armor of ghostly silver behind the tamer plants.

The girl retreated soundlessly, turned on her heel, and flew toward the path by the elderberries. When she darted a look just before plunging onto the path, the two were motionless, the boy lying close against his mother's heart.

She ran pell-mell down the rut until she tired, the breath sawing painfully in and out her throat. How loggy with sleep she was! Her legs felt lumbering and disconnected from the rest of her body. The packed dirt jarred her feet. It seemed as if she had never adapted to passing quickly and quietly along the ridge trails. When she stopped, a valley of mist lay before her, impossibly wide and deep. Leaning against the trunk of a tree, she cried briefly, feeling the immensities of the world and the disorder of the night and morning.

A hand brushed her shoulder, and she shrieked and spun around.

"Lang! You scared me!"

Her brother laughed, looking jaunty and handsome, with a sprig of purple monkshood stuck behind one ear.

"I was off scanning the hills for the daughter of the house," he said grandly. "Questing for Our Lady of the Rain. No such luck."

"You weren't! That's a fearful——"

"I paid Miss Sally to let us stay one more night. And bought some food as well. You know, we could use a rest. That was a nice soft featherbed."

"It wasn't feathers at all, except the pallet right on top. Underneath it was nothing but cornshucks. Musty. Old. Shucks." Ingledove felt a sharp dismay. How could he consider sleeping in that chamber another night? "I don't think Danagasta would approve. That girl. There's something the matter with her. Normal people don't wander around in thunderstorms or float in and stare at their houseguests. Sally called Ild a *wilding*, something untamable maybe, and *she* must be like him. There's another thing; she didn't look the same as the first time I—"

Lang had been whistling, one hand over his eyes as he scanned the slopes opposite, but here he interrupted her with a protest.

"What could be wrong with her? Mind, I think the boy and the mother a bit spooky. Fey. Or mad. But Mrs. Bristly-Lip likes the money, and she keeps a clean house. A day of rest would be good. After all, we'll have to start for home in a week. Maybe two. We're a good march from Hazel Creek, and even when we make it there, we'll have a ways to travel."

She plucked a stem of flowering grass and nervously tore it to bits. Her brother was not going to listen to her. She could tell that he'd made up his mind to get a better look at the pretty stranger.

"I think the lady might be . . ."

"What?"

"Dangerous. I'm afraid of her. For that matter, I'm a little scared of Sally."

Lang hooted. "Afraid of a backcountry dummern with a mustache? That's silly."

"I'm afraid of your Lady who wafts in without anybody see-

ing how and disappears the same way. I'm afraid of somebody
who likes to prance about in storms, dodging lightning bolts.
Get it? Or maybe she can handle an electrical charge. She's
more than strange. I'm absolutely sure of that," Ingledove finished in a rush, tugging at her brother's arm.

He began paring a hazel twig with his knife, letting the
peels fall into the grass.

"You've got the world going tailfirst and your boots in the
clouds," he replied. "She's just a mountain belle, no more and
no less. The family's odd, sure, and she may be, too. The old
witch wouldn't even tell me her own daughter's name when
I asked. But nobody who is dangerous has a smile like that
one."

"Oh, Lang," his sister whispered. There was no use. What
he decided would be the last word. They would sleep another
night in the cabin. He would try to catch sight of his Lady of
the Rain, maybe go walking hand in hand with her down the
lonely ridgetop path . . .

The hours lifted and floated away, and there was no sign of
her. Ingledove felt caught between her apprehension of the
coming darkness and her relief that the young woman in the
white gown had not materialized in the clearing. She and
Lang washed their clothes in the kettle with ash soap, and they
baked bread in Sally's oven. The day began to feel ordinary, as
if domestic tasks could drive out the uncanny and keep them
safe.

In late afternoon the brother and sister perched on a
cracked and lichened boulder in the middle of the clearing. A
soot-black star marked where lightning had slammed against
the stone during the night.

"You stand guard duty, since you're so loath to close your eyes with weird Sally and her children around." Lang was teasing, but in a few minutes he was fast asleep, lying with one arm curled around his head. Ingledove gazed at him for a while; he was as handsome as a snowy marble statue dug from the flank of a Greek hill. When he couldn't talk back and make jokes of her fears, he seemed a very good sort of brother. Ild and Sally were out of sight, napping in the cabin, and the girl felt utterly alone. The rock was hard, the air motionless except for some doodling midges, and the whole panorama from mountaintop to distant valleys was a woven green, with hardly so much as a brown stitch that might indicate another cabin. Stretching out at full length, chin propped in her hands, she brooded on the solitude of the place. How she would have welcomed the distant sound of a church bell, the clattering of a train, the shouts of children playing tag! The sun was as pale as frost, half-extinguished by cloud and beginning to sink. It was a time of day that usually held charm for Ingledove, when daily cares were over and the firm outlines of the world seemed to waver and slide into the mystery of dusk. The crooked boughs of the laurel hell formed a dense tangle at the sides of the clearing—the big catawba rhododendrons were past their flowering, and the leaves hung dark and leathery. From the prominence where she sat, the valley on one side fell away in jerks like the trajectory of a woman tumbling and catching herself as she plummeted toward sleep. Clouds, collecting above a stream thousands of feet below, hushed noise. Once a white-eyed vireo flew out of an oak and back like a toy boomerang. It seemed to stress the stillness of the hour by its brief flight, so quickly past.

The heat radiating from the slab of stone made her sleepy, and she pillowed her head on one arm. She wouldn't give in to drowsiness, however; she was too strongly determined. But what was that sound? She could make out an elaborate dripping and trickling—the spring where they had collected water for the pot, joined with splashes from far away. Drifting on the intricate song, she closed her eyes. Then, diving toward unconsciousness, she felt alarm; confused and unclear in import, it was enough to make her fly the valley of sleep. She sat up, heart thumping.

The Lady of the Rain had come into the clearing.

Though her eyes were on Lang, she slowly turned her head and gave Ingledove one sidelong glance. The gown she wore was thin and close-fitting, rather like the ones Danagasta had made but narrower and glistening. Around her neck hung a bell without a clapper, a tiny flared cup as black as obsidian. The girl well remembered the features and the windings and loops of hair, but now she felt a deep horror of the pale figure. The wide-set eyes, the delicate nose, and the slender mouth could only be called lovely, and yet something in the young woman's aspect told her that in this being was no drop of life sympathetic to her own. She instinctively recoiled from her, as swiftly as she would have rejected a snowy angel of death shedding its spores beside a windfall oak.

"What are you?" she whispered.

The Lady did not reply, though she drew closer until her shadow fell like a bar across Lang's brow.

"I don't know who you are, and maybe I don't want to know. Leave us alone." Ingledove got onto her knees, one arm stretched above the unconscious face, to shield it from shadow and stare. As if in response, her brother shifted in sleep, so that the star made a dark corona around his head.

A smile twitched at the stranger's lips; then the sleeper woke and rubbed his eyes. With an exclamation he sprang from the hard bed and laughed with pleasure.

"Lang, no—"

"Our Lady of the Rain," he said, reaching for the long fingers.

"No—"

She wondered whether the fingertips felt as cold as she imagined, as blighting to the touch. Helpless to prevent what her brother desired, she stood on the riven stone and saw him lean to whisper. The pair of them looked slantwise at her. He still had hold of the Lady's hand! And she nodded, amused by whatever he was saying. Ingledove clenched her fists, nails sharp against her palms, as the young woman lowered her lids, looking modestly at the ground.

"Say!" There was the mother, bellowing from the door.

The Lady of the Rain laughed, lazily, her hand moving through the air in what might have been meant as a wave or as a placating gesture. Whatever the movement was, it silenced Sally.

She turned away and touched Lang on the chest, speaking to him in a low voice. Then, gathering up her skirts, she darted across the yard and disappeared through a gap in the laurel.

"Wait . . ."

Following quickly, he ducked through the opening but was back almost instantly.

"It's tight going." He stood with head cocked, staring at the cramped space between the boughs. "She must be really slim to wriggle through so quickly."

"Or perhaps it's something else entirely. Have you thought of that?" Ingledove looked at her brother's hand, as if she suspected it might be marked by the taint of a toxin. "What is she? Not rain but storm and lightning and not Lady but—"

"Don't be so peculiar." He smiled, his eyes still on the crooked laurel branches. "She said I could call her Malia. It doesn't seem like a mountain name to me. I wonder where Old Bristly-Lip got that one?"

It was hours before the girl could put away thoughts of the strange young woman who had lured her brother to follow so easily. In the morning they would leave; already she had made him promise that he would not linger another day. And it seemed that Sally did not want them. She had gone into the inner room and shut the door. Now and then they could hear Ild's voice, protesting against bedtime. Tonight the way to outside had been sealed and barred. Already it was stuffy and warm in the cabin, unpleasant for sleeping.

All the same, Ingledove was too exhausted to stay awake and dropped off while her brother was cutting bread and dried meat for sandwiches. Perhaps it was the humid air or the smell of soot and salt hams hanging from the ceiling, but she dreamed of fire and drops of water rising in burning clouds. The cabin was flaming, and she was trying to rescue the little boy, reaching in the window and grasping for his hand. He went on crying as if broken-hearted, without any attempt to save himself. At last she grabbed hold of an arm and wrenched him up to the windowsill, but when she glimpsed a face it was not his at all but Malia's—and not weeping but grinning—so she let go and fell head over heels off the ridge, somersaulting toward the valley floor.

She woke, shrieking, sodden with sweat, and reached for Lang. At once she saw that he was gone, and the flood of wordless song was back, pouring through the flung-open door. Shivering, Ingledove crawled from bed and hurried to it, rushing from the dim cabin into the clearing. The scene was overpowering, for a wind had blown the clouds away from the stars and waning moon, and the sky, unimpeded by the lights of hamlets and towns, blazed like a phosphorescent sea. The ridgetop seemed to have been thrust nearer the heavens, so that the flaming stars were bigger, looking gelid and swollen in the moist air: the fiery zodiac and the heroes and goddesses of the ancient world appeared to have come unpinned and to be sinking toward earth.

Racing to the lip of the clearing, Ingledove almost collided with Sally, who was hunched over a path, swinging a light. Beams bobbed along the dirt, but there was no sign of anyone else.

"Take it," the woman offered, and the barefoot girl accepted the lantern and hurried from the yard.

"Lang! Lang! Lang!" echoed from the hillsides as the constellations wheeled just above and seemed to stare with all their might. Tripping, nicking her feet on shards, sliding on muddy patches, Ingledove pushed farther and farther. The delirious cascade of notes seemed to leap from every direction, echoing and reechoing from the heights. She might have missed him if she had not stopped so often to catch her breath; she could hardly hear over the song and the blood rushing in her ears. And if not for the dazzling swirl of stars she would never have seen him, lying discarded at the edge of a laurel hell, his shirt torn. He was barely moaning, unconscious of her approach. She could not lift him. He rolled his eyes and tried to lie down when she tugged him to a sitting position.

"Lang, help me, help me," she entreated, but it was no use.

Finally she gave up and went away, leaving the flickering lamp to mark the place. She climbed to the clearing more slowly than she had come, gasping and gulping for air and sometimes crying. Breath was a moving knife blade, metallic to the taste. A fresh lantern shone near the door and showed Sally's head poking from the cabin. Was she ready to jump inside her burrow and bar the way? The full-throated song burgeoned, battering their ears.

"It's me," Ingledove called hoarsely. She bent and rested, hands on knees, panting.

Closing the door, the woman came to meet her. She asked nothing, seemed to expect no news beyond the rising tide of notes that threatened to drown the world in melody.

"I found him. I need help. To get him here."

Silently Sally nodded and went to retrieve the candle lantern. There was no surprise on her face—no expression, really. At the path she cast a glance toward the cabin and then followed so slowly that Ingledove could have danced and howled like an imp. The fear that her brother would have vanished was upon her, leaning on her chest like Danagasta's night rider, but he was still there by the guttering candle, flung on his side next to the laurel roots. It took the rescuers a long time to persuade him onto his feet and stagger to the clearing. At the edge of the scrub he collapsed.

"Drag him," Sally said with a grim determination, reaching for an arm. Candles out, the pair of lanterns clanked as they swung from her belt.

They pulled him across the moss and the wildflowers, soaking his back.

"Sobby wet ground." Now the stronger of the two stopped to rest, hands on hips. With a quick intake of breath she knelt and pulled at the neck of his shirt.

"What's that?" Ingledove bent over, staring at the red welts below his collarbone. "What's the matter with him?" Her voice rose, teetered uncertainly.

"Maybe a snake," the other muttered, looking around the cabin site.

"Will he be all right? Can you help him?"

"I can poultice it. You'll have to get him to walk. The Witchmaster's the one you need. And that's a fair piece of trudging from here."

The girl wiped away tears with her hem. Danagasta had mentioned a witchmaster, hadn't she? "I've heard of him, but I don't know the way."

"I can point you, but that's all." Sally shoved her arms under Lang's and heaved him upward.

It took considerable wrestling to get him over the doorsill and onto the bed, where he lay like the dead with his eyes rolled out of sight. Ingledove clutched at his hand, wondering how they could ever find the man called the Witchmaster and make it home again. And what if Lang didn't recover—if he died? She would never be brave enough to hike the long way to Hazel Creek alone and then cross the drowned lands in the periwinkle boat, which they had so carefully hidden under brush. The song might dog her steps, and she wasn't sure she could endure the terror of the big spaces of the wilderness if every gap resounded with the lyrical, treacherous-seeming voice. For the first time in her life, she thought about what it might feel like to go mad, every speck of reason washed away by a tsunami of fear and song. And she couldn't stand it here, though tonight Sally had given her a help that was priceless and a kind of rough sympathy—and was even now busy lighting the lanterns, fetching herbs and linen bandages, a bowl of water. But when the woman went to the inner room for a clean cloth, she cried out and emerged almost instantly, lips pressed tight together.

"What's the matter?"

"It's Ild."

"Is he sick? Is he gone?"

The mother nodded, her hand going to the silver cross. "Lit out. Got past us in the laurel, maybe. Or been took. He's nothing but a stray woodscolt, but he's dear. Sweet God. I can't . . ."

Already Ingledove was pulling socks onto her sore and muddy feet. She didn't let herself consider one way or another. There wasn't a choice. She knew she lacked any skill with the bunches of herbs arranged on the bed. She could do no more than wash her brother, and that would be of no use. Perhaps nothing would help, but she had to let someone else try. It was their fault—hers and, more so, Lang's—that the little boy had been left alone.

Lantern in hand, she paused, looking at Sally, who stared at her face a long moment before speaking.

"Go, then . . ."

Running to the door, Ingledove dived into the immense shining, singing night. "Ild, Ild, Ild," she called, her head buzzing with weariness. Again she followed the path that wound below the ridgetop. Past the root that curled like a huge turban in the path, across the balancing stone, through the archway in the laurel. At last she came around a jag of path and saw him, standing fearlessly on a promontory of rock. Whether he stared into the abyss of the valley with its white fume of clouds or at the disorderly brilliance of the stars, she could not tell. She felt a terror at the thought of the boy hanging over the deep, and it was accentuated by the vast mountains standing in massed rows, barely visible against the sky.

"Ild," she called softly, so as not to startle him.

He peered over his shoulder, then came to her readily. She shuddered as he slipped his hand into hers and smiled, the starlight glinting on his small, close-set teeth.

"Why did you go?"

"I heard the singing. I was looking." His eyes widened and his eyebrows shot up comically, as if surprised she needed to ask, as if his words explained only the obvious.

She led him all the way home, not even letting go when he seesawed in play on the teetering stone. She was too tired to lose anybody again. When they reached the yard, Sally dashed out the cabin door, and Ild scampered to meet her and sprang into her arms.

She rocked him, one hand supporting his head, as Ingledove came forward.

"He'll mend." The woman nodded toward the dark house. "At least for traveling."

At the doorway Ingledove paused to glance back. The two were still embracing on the stage of the clearing with the lights of the universe upon them and the ecstatic voice ringing in their ears. It was as mysterious as a dream . . . The image blurred, and with a sudden jerk she stopped herself from falling. She felt as if she'd waked to something else, too, because she understood finally that not only did Sally love the boy and he her but there was something between them that was essential to the happiness of each—even despite the fact that one of them also feared the other. For an instant she remembered Ild on the plank of stone above the abyss and then imagined the mother's vigil by candlelight, praying, crying, washing somebody else's boy. She couldn't help picturing a tall white figure beside the bed, but whether it was an angel of comfort or destruction, she didn't know. Perhaps it would be Malia. In a moment she would drop onto the coverlet and sleep beside Lang, seemingly as dead as he, though not the same—an unknown struggle was already going on inside him, and the poison might be gathering under the poultice. Never had she been so exhausted. She had to ask now, had to know before she gave in and collapsed in sleep.

"About your daughter," she began.

Sally's arms stiffened around Ild, and she stood up, grasping both his hands in hers. "That's outlander thinking. Can't you tell? That's no daughter of mine."

Lost

It seemed as though the voice had called every last cloud from the sky, for in the morning the ridge and the valleys were socked in, and Ingledove could hardly see Sally and Ild when she turned to wave. In her hand was a crude map, drawn on a sheet of coarse, floury paper that once must have been a sack. A mass of winding lines marked mountain streams and paths so thick with landmarks that the girl hoped she could not get lost. One piece of luck was theirs; they were no more than a rough day's hike from the Witchmaster. Lang was subdued and weak but willing to set out early. He remembered nothing of the night before; he had looked carefully at the injury in the cabin's one mirror, strung over a nail on the parlor wall, his eyes going to his sister's but his expression remaining unreadable.

"My own doing," he had told her, unsmiling. "I guess that's what you're thinking. And you'd be right."

"I'm just thinking about the man Sally calls the Witchmaster. That's all." And it was true; the anger she might have felt had been burned up in the fire of her fear for Lang and for Ild. So she had put her arms around her older brother and had laid her head on his shoulder, away from the wound. "I just want you to be well."

"Me too." The voice had been tremulous, but he had pressed one hand against her shoulder blade, good and hard.

They passed the spot where she had discovered his body the night before, and Ingledove saw a shred of linen snagged on a twig. Some day next spring, birds hunting in the laurel hells would tug the threads free, she thought, not mentioning the place to Lang. She had to run and help him over the seesawing rock; he was tallow-pale, and sweat beaded on his forehead. Or maybe it was just a smattering of cloud, sweeping against his face. This morning she was carrying most of the supplies in her pack, while his held nothing but a little bedding and the oiled canvas fly, lashed on top. It was more difficult than she had realized, bearing the extra weight. Perhaps she should go back and leave what they had at the cabin. But what if they didn't find the Witchmaster? What if they got lost without food or shelter?

By the end of the second hour, Ingledove was anxious. Fearing that she had made the wrong choice, she suggested that they pause to rest and drink the sweet tea that Sally had poured into a chipped glass container. It didn't help; stopping made nothing clear, and Lang dropped to sleep instantly, curled on his side. He hadn't even bothered to remove the pack. She perched on a stone, eyes on his face, which appeared shiny, coated with a thin layer of oily sweat. Since she had rationed herself to an inch of liquid, refreshment was soon at an end. After fifteen minutes she woke her brother, patting his cheeks until his eyes opened. She was afraid to shake him, to do anything that might irritate the wound.

"Here, have a drink." She held out the jar. He drained it quickly before she could prevent him from drinking so much. He needed it, she reasoned. It was all right. "We have to move faster," she told him, not sure whether he could.

"I can do that. I'm just a little drowsy." He staggered, getting onto his feet, but immediately set off, as if to prove that he was able.

Before noon they came to a wide gap in the laurel where the trail split, one fork zigzagging steeply upward, the other slipping more easily along the foot of a ridge.

"Take the left fork," Ingledove murmured, studying the map. "That's good."

But not long afterward she found a rude cairn that was not on the map. There the path divided again.

"I like that one," Lang said suddenly, pointing to a log over a stream that rushed through low flat stones and fled clear and quicksilver-fleet over pebbles and the glint of fool's gold. The way looked neither more nor less logical than the other choice, which hugged the opposite bank.

The girl examined his face. "You don't feel something influencing you? You don't hear a voice—do you?"

"I don't know what you mean. An influence like the stars? It just seems pleasant there, with the ferns and those frothy-looking flowers hanging over the creek."

"I don't know what I mean either. It's just that last night was so disturbing . . ."

For several miles they followed the increasingly narrow path until it petered out in a scrubby meadow. The brother and sister stared into a swath of wildflowers. Ingledove forced herself to breathe slowly, but she was alarmed. A stand of bee balm glowed in the sunlight, the blossoms topped by the golden fuzz of bees and by swallowtails, tilting extravagant wings as they fed. One lifted up and wobbled away, flitting across the open ground in loops of lovely, wasteful flight. Watching its prodigal scattering of energy, she felt calmer and lowered her pack to the earth.

"Sorry," Lang said.

She counted to ten and sat down before nodding, her back aching. She wondered whether it had been worth the extra walk to hear her brother apologize. Twice in one day he had admitted error, she thought—highly singular acts. He looked a little better, the brisk walk having restored color to his cheeks, although it seemed that he should feel worse, as she did.

"What am I thinking!" He bent and began tugging on the straps to his sister's rucksack. "How about my compass? Unless we've left it behind. We could cut cross-country and try to meet up with a trail on the sketch . . ."

Dumping out the contents of the heavy pack, he pawed through the foodstuffs and clothes. His companion watched without attempting to rise, feeling only a flicker of interest.

"Here it is!" He appeared pleased for the first time in hours, until it occurred to him that he didn't know the compass directions for their previous wandering. "But maybe we can guess what to do, based on the approximate distance and the direction of the light as we walked here."

A guess hadn't worked the first time, Ingledove thought. And who could remember where the sun had been at each stage of the day—before, behind, to one side or the other? But she let him putter with his notebook and pencil and compass. She was used to letting him do as he wished. Drowsiness had worked its way into her bones. "Wake me in ten minutes," she told him, then pillowed her head on a bedroll and drifted off to sleep.

She doubted whether he had actually let her rest for more than an instant, as it seemed that no sooner had her cheek touched cloth than he'd begun shaking her by the shoulder. Her burden was more unwieldy and weighty than before, she felt sure, less compactly arranged. When she checked Sally's drawing, she found that a number of confusing dotted lines had been added as proposed routes. "It's as though he *wants* to get lost," she thought, staring at the smeared scribbles. Still, Lang led them, gripping his compass. Ingledove was growing so weary that she felt each step as a jolt. Her very teeth felt jarred.

"Maybe we should make camp here and spend the night," her brother suggested after they had scrambled up the flank of a ridge. It had been fast-paced and wretched going, with slippery shale underfoot. Twice she had fallen, scraping her leg above the boot. She had begun to wonder which one of them was ill, for her blood seemed as slothful as molasses—as if she were the one who had been poisoned. It was Lang who had gotten a new lease on energy and was moving more surely. They were taking another break because of her.

"No, no, I don't want to do that." Sleeping outside was the furthest thing from what she had planned. What she hoped for was a roof over their heads. If the singing began, she wanted strong walls between them and the voice. Why she feared it, she still was not sure, but it had to do with the song's link to the site where she had seen Malia, the girl who was not Sally's daughter. With bitterness the woman had confessed that she was barren and had never been able to give her "old man" a child. Now he was dead. And she did not know the young woman, not even so much as a name, though she had seen her pass through the clearing before and thought her an apparition. Each time the pale figure had made an appearance, Ild had tried to follow; perhaps she lured him. Yet he was afraid as well, the poor little boy whom his foster mother had found naked and screaming convulsively on her doorstep, a foot of umbilical cord still tied to his belly. "Some girl with a bad man who done her dirty, and her dropping a woodscolt in the laurel." That was Sally's reading of events. Maybe she knew or feared more; maybe something stopped her mouth.

No, Ingledove didn't want to stay here. "Help us, Messenger of Fire and Cloud who guides the lost," she whispered. Danagasta, who had cautioned her to call on this being by name, was the one who had pointed out its starry home, sometimes burning, sometimes wreathed in milky cloud. The girl had never grasped exactly what it was—an angel come golden from the heavenly throne? She had imagined that a comet would zing toward earth in a single-minded curve like a flung arrow.

"What did you say?" Lang was smiling, nervously tossing a fragment of quartz from hand to hand. He appeared almost himself, only a faint sheen on his face reminding her of this morning's pallor. He was again the strong and handsome boy whom the other fellows wanted on school teams—the one the girls watched, gazing over a shoulder for a second too long. Perhaps Sally was nothing but an ignorant mountain woman, fearful and prone to make every injury into a tragedy.

"There's a mosquito on your neck . . ." Ingledove flicked aside the loose opening of his shirt. Closing her eyes, she swayed back and forth, feeling suddenly queasy and wishing she had not seen the blue-black skin. The bite marks, swollen shut, seemed only dimples.

"What did you say?" He repeated the words more slowly this time.

"Let's eat some dried meat. Then we'll feel stronger."

"I'm not even hungry," he protested.

She looked at him curiously. How could he not be hungry? Was he just putting up a front, or had the poison done something to his appetite? He appeared fresh and able to go much farther. "Well, I am," she said, reaching for the pack.

"Listen," he whispered.

Although positive that she could hear the faraway song for one hair-raising instant, she soon realized that this was something else entirely. She made out a snatch of sung words, then a pause in which she strained to hear anything—and another tune began, this one much closer and jauntier.

"Help! Help! Heeeelp!"

"Calm down," Lang said when she paused for breath. He was looking annoyed, his pencil tapping against the home-made map.

She stared at her brother. His pupils were just pinpoints, and once again she noticed that his skin seemed slick. She remembered stories of changelings, how the fairies would steal a child and leave a false staring thing in its bed. But that happened to babies and beautiful small children, didn't it? "Tam Lin," she murmured. Tam Lin was the knight on the milk-white steed who was turned into a snake and a deer and a hot iron in the fire before brave Janet could rescue him from the Fairy Queen. That was mad, though, to think that way. The Queen was cruel, and in her anger wished that she had given Tam Lin a heart like a cobble and eyes of tree. That was so arresting—*eyes of tree*. Ingledove had begged Danagasta to repeat that stanza, over and over, the first time she had sung that song.

"Hush, hush. We don't know who that is." Lang was gripping her arm, whispering close to her ear.

The girl drew away from him. "What's wrong with you? You could die if you don't get help! You want to be lost!"

"That's silly." He frowned at her. "That's just not true. I feel stronger than I have all day. In fact, I really feel better than before. More than I usually do. Honest. Probably I just tripped and knocked my head in the dark, and yes, something bit me. But it wasn't a poisonous viper, as you and old Sally seemed to think. Or else I'd be dead, wouldn't I?"

Before he had finished speaking Ingledove began hollering for help again. She peered over the ridge, where she could see leaves rustling as if something huge were moving parallel to the top. This time when the singing began, she could make out the words clearly.

A dauncy doodlebug so fair
Was prancing in the summer air.

A wildmire in a sarvice tree
Said, "Silverbell, please marry me."

"How should I love, and I so young?"
The mincy doodlebug among

The blooming blossom-bushes cried.
"Bodaciously," the mire replied,

"So pearten up, my doney gal,
And be the Mistress of Sir Tal,

We'll play all day at Wheavilly Wheat,
And after dance the shoo-fly neat—

"Help!" Rocks began to slide under her feet, and she hastily sat down and leaned over the edge. "Heeelp! Help! Somebody help me! Help!"

"You'll make yourself hoarse." Lang had followed her and was standing idly by. He looked a little angry, his eyes narrowed.

She ignored him and kept yelling with all her might.

"Halloo!" A redheaded boy emerged from the trees below and waved a staff at her. "I'm a-coming," he shouted, jumping with a will from boulder to boulder and stabbing his stick into the ground.

As he hopped closer, Ingledove gaped in surprise.

"That's the tallest boy I've ever seen," her brother said, showing interest for the first time.

And he was oversized. *Big* wasn't big enough for his

britches—he was positively mighty, with great hands and feet and a massive, friendly face centered around a generous nose pocked by pimples. He ran the last treacherous wall of stone before vaulting over the top.

Slamming his palms together, he called out, "Messer's my name, witchmaster's my game. What's the rumpus?" He grinned, showing a parade of crooked, mossy teeth.

Ingledove stood up, shaking slightly but filled with a welling relief. Nothing could be too far gone with this large friendliness on their side.

THE BOY WITCHMASTER

"Scratched by a briar." The Witchmaster made the sign of the cross, and his eyes stayed fixed on the blackened skin with the two faint dimples for a long time.

"That's what Danagasta said! *Scratched by a briar*—remember?"

Lang shook his head. For the first time he seemed nervous about the injury. Perhaps he had forced himself to ignore the wound; perhaps that was simple enough, since it was hard for him to make out the site, so high on his chest, almost at his collarbone. They had no mirror.

"Sally said it was a snake," he ventured.

"Hush. That ain't snakebite. If it'd been a rattler, say, above your heart like that, you'd be dead." The giant boy let out an explosive sigh. "I can't do no good with this." He stared toward the faraway mountains, which by daylight in blowing mist resembled the pale green of talc stone. Farther on they faded to blue. "It's gone beyond the lights of Knox Messer. I'm nothing but an apprentice, really. I'm no witchmaster, not yet. But I'm the first Messer to be made a witchmaster in three generations."

"I don't know about that—I don't know anything about witchmasters," Ingledove said, feeling desperate. "A woman named Sally told us to search for the Witchmaster, and she gave us these directions, but we got lost." She showed him the crumpled paper with its wavering, hard-to-follow lines.

Knox let out a hoot as he surveyed the map. "Looks like chicken scratchings to me. I know who you mean—Sally Shelby. She sits right spang on a ridgetop, where there ain't much of a neighbor, with that woods brat she found in the laurel."

"Yes, that must be the one. But what do we do now?" Sitting, she stretched out her legs, wanting to yank off her leather boots but sure she would never be able to force them back on if she did. There was a spot at each heel that burned like a broken blister—she didn't think she could stand the stinging much longer.

"She never meant for you to find *me*. She wanted the one we call the Master of Witchmasters. He's over the rest of us, as much as the sun is over tin sluts of burning grease."

"A slut," Lang repeated; "that's a homemade lamp, isn't it?"

Knox drew his big head back, eyeing them both.

"What's your names—the family names, I mean—your ma and pap and their parents?"

Ingledove told him. She had given up and was unlacing the boots. Maybe she could bandage her feet somehow.

"Well, your ma was Adantan right enough," he mused. "I know her names from the Tree of Life. But not you two—no young'uns. Where you been? I never saw your features afore. But you're dressed right. Something out of plumb here, I reckon."

A tear spilled from the girl's eye, and she wiped it away angrily. Her feet were blotchy, and the heels were a mass of broken blisters and blood. It had soaked her socks. Why had they come? Why had she listened to her brother? Danagasta had betrayed them, urging them to cross the reservoir. No, that wasn't true—it wasn't her fault that Lang had wanted to go on and on, feeling the freedom of summer in the mountains. He was to blame. He wasn't even caring about what he had done. He had wandered off and appeared to be daydreaming, his head cocked. Maybe he was listening to some sparrows chittering in an ash tree.

"What's the Tree of Life? What's *Adantan*? What's a daughter of Adantis? I don't know anything you're talking about." Her voice sounded not so much angry as strung with tears.

"*Ku!* Would you look!" Knox delicately turned her foot and examined the raw skin. "I can help with that." He began pawing in a sack that had hung over his shoulder. Out came strips of willow bark, a bunch of alumroot, a two-pronged hazel stick that he said was a divining rod, a coarse-woven bag full of jack-in-the-pulpit corms, and a jumble of tiny vials swaddled in rags to keep them from clinking together.

"Do you mind?" He broke a beeswax seal on one of the bottles and began smearing salve on Ingledove's heels.

"What is that?"

"There's willow, some mashed spring grubs, zinc, calendula, a bit of enchanter's nightshade. Smells like wintergreen, so there's some of that, too. This was compounded by the fellow you're looking for. It's good."

"Grubs! That's disgusting! But you know the way, then." She felt a sprig of hope. "And you didn't answer my questions."

Rubbing his hands together until the traces of ointment vanished, Knox grinned. "Yes, ma'am. Can't do everything at once. And you didn't tell me where you came from, either. Lessee. *The Tree of Life* is Adantan genealogy. Every witchmaster has to know the families and recognize the names."

"But what's *Adantan*?" She felt impatient. "What's *Witchmaster*? What's 'daughter of Adantis'? That's what somebody chiseled on Marm's marker, down at the base of the stone. Why?" She sighed, sweeping her hand across the grass-stained linen skirt and thinking how Danagasta would reprove her. "I'm being rude, aren't I? Thank you for the medicine. It's very soothing, even if there are squashed grubs in it."

"Here," he said, passing her another container. "Drink this. You don't need to thank me. You'll help somebody else, another day."

She looked with suspicion at the orange-red contents.

"No grubs, I promise. It won't hurt you. I use this all the time when I'm journeying: Jarrett's Special Tonic for Travelers. Now, I don't remember exactly what's in that mixture, except there's bloodroot that makes it go that color."

"I thought bloodroot was poisonous," Ingledove murmured, tilting the little vessel and holding it to the light. The sides were thick and bubbly; the bottle must have been handmade. Hadn't she been warned against the heart-shaped leaves with deep-cut lobes and the frail flowers? There was a bed of them in the garden at home, and every spring after they had bloomed, Danagasta watched the plants until the seeds ripened, then bent the bulging pods and buried them in the damp ground. Sometimes the thinning shells tore and the seed spilled, the slick black winks jumping onto the ground and rolling away. But she would hunt for each, dibbling a shallow hole and covering it over, watering the soil afterward.

"A lot of medicines are poisonous," Knox said cheerfully. "Or else they wouldn't have any virtue. It's just like people, whether Adantan or foreign. There's bad and good stirred together, and one or the other has the upper hand. Sometimes both at the same time. A dip of some poisons can't hurt."

She drank it off, though the taste was sharp and unpleasant.

"Your own ma, was it, buried over Hazel Creek way?"

Ingledove nodded.

"Well, it's like this: she was born in Adantis, and I guess she married out. That's pretty rare. Most Adantans don't want to roost with outlanders. But she didn't disremember home, and maybe she wanted a recollection of it at her grave. If there was anybody to tell."

"Danagasta," she whispered. She wanted her just then; wanted to ask if Marm had talked about the past, about family. Hadn't she said something about wanting to go home, there at the end? She couldn't quite remember. "But what is Adantis? I still don't understand."

"You're in it. There's foreigners who think it's theirs, or their government's, but the land's Adantis."

"Who's we?"

"Some say the Hidden People. The History Tellers say that many of our forepeople were from around the Irish Sea, from Scotland and northern England and northern Ireland. Here they became what's called branch-water people, living high up in the mountains, and they mingled with the Cherokee who hid out about the time of the Removal. The Trail of Tears. Others trickled in later—mostly the muley-hawed ones that just couldn't abide a government and doted on the old ways. It's a nation of us, with our own secret boundaries. It's got all the wildest kind of mountain lands in what you call Carolina and Tennessee and even a scrap of Georgia. We stray into the outer regions, now and then. Not me—I'm too tall and peart to sneak by. But we have to keep up, so we can pass for outlandish if we need to; mostly we just live on the dodge and never meet any. We don't want to be the same as them. We talk English, but we know a smattering of Cherokee words and names from Mooney. The Witchmaster says that the Old Worlders were already a mixed-up people, even before Adantis—Celts overrun by Romans, then by Saxons, then Vikings and the Irish, and last by the Normans. When the Cherokee and the border peoples mixed together, they made a new thing out of the shamanism of the Indians mated with the godly and witchmaster beliefs of the Old World borderers." He had been groping in the bottom of his poke and now brandished a roll of white linen in triumph. Though stained by herbs, it appeared clean enough and felt soothing, strapped around ankle and under foot.

"Mooney," she prompted.

"He wrote two of our books that tell the passed-down lore. Everybody has Mooney and the Bible to read."

Knox stared at Lang, who was pacing restlessly, his head still tilted. Maybe he had been eavesdropping. Maybe he was listening to a more distant voice. "I'd like to make him some dittany tea," he murmured. "It's healthful for bites. Snakebite, anyway. But I ain't got none with me. Probably wouldn't have no merit."

He began packing his bag. "What about *my* question? About where you came from? You didn't say."

Ingledove pleated a piece of fabric between her fingers, wondering if she dared ask him to guide her to the Master of Witchmasters' house. "We grew up here and there along Hazel Creek, but men came and burned the towns when I was little, and then they flooded the valley. And now there's nothing left but graveyards above the reservoir."

"The drowned lands. Government doings. I know that place. And your ma is buried there."

"Yes. Before that our father had gone off to make his fortune in South America, but he never came back. So the man Marm worked for took us in for good, and Danagasta cared for us."

"Danagasta. That's an Adantan name."

"I didn't know. I always thought that she had sensed we needed her. Like magic. Because she just appeared when my mother took sick."

Knox looked at her but didn't tell what he was thinking.

"What about my brother? Can you do anything more for him? What about the salve?" Drawing up her knees, she lapped the hem of her skirt over her sore feet. "I already feel better. I think I could walk a lot farther." She wasn't really sure about that, but it made her more confident to say it.

"I don't reckon you should be hoofing it anywhere, unless you go barefoot—though your feet are probably too soft." He glanced across at Lang. "Why don't you tell me everything that happened from before you left home until he got bit?"

And so she did, starting with the nightmare that had alarmed Danagasta. Knox sat cross-legged on the ground, his eyes drifting across the slopes opposite as he listened to the story of how they had departed, crossed the drowned lands, visited the graves, and wandered in the mountains, stumbling across Sally, Ild, and Malia. By the time she had finished, Lang was curled on a rock in the sun.

"You need the one above all the other witchmasters in Adantis," Knox told her again. He tugged at his ponytail twist of red hair. "He can cure inward spiritual harms; he compasses the old backcountry magic—sorcery and charms and such. He's met the devilish things in the shadow places that were here before the Adantans were, and the creatures that were brought in the bellies of ships more than two centuries ago, some of them. He's studied with learned masters over the sea. He knows, and he's a right-minded man."

Ingledove felt wide-awake but strange—as if her blood might be wheeling through her body a little faster than usual.

"Nothing that has happened since we camped at Hazel Creek has made sense. How do you mean—things that were brought, that are devilish? It's not like this at home."

"Well, the wild blustery places draw strange beasts. They'd be bored in somebody's warehouse or shop or parlor, trammeled by manners. They'd probably eat up everybody and hightail it home! And the ancient lairs of monsters and the sites where the Cherokee mother towns stood are magnetic. Adantans say that their Old World ancestors were so long used to nesting with mysteries that their great-great-great-grandchildren lure the creatures. Such beings just belong in Adantis. But they can cause rimpshions of trouble.

"And the old ones, who could discern the creatures better than we, told our great-great-great-grandmarms that there were stowaways in the ships. So many chances for escape, ship after ship plowing lickety-cut to the New World from Carrickfergus and Londonderry and Ayr, Morecambe and Kirkcudbright and secret pirate ports in the cliffs that nobody even remembers anymore.

"There's a story my great-grandmarm Knox told me about a ship called the *Serpent & Eagle*. Right from the very evening outen the harbor, the captain worried that there was something wrong and slantdicular about the journey. He had the men hunting for a stowaway, but the boat was jammed with passengers, and nobody found anything peculiar. But the captain knew, and he didn't like it. Then sailors got to disappearing—one, then another, until five were missing and they'd had to recruit a couple of Scottish farmers to help. Paid 'em high, too, because the people belowdecks were afraid."

Knox paused, his eyes on the wavelike ridges.

"Now and then the captain would spy out a lady in a sea-colored gown, singing sadly and looking across the bow, but when he'd go to speak, she'd be melted away into the shadows. And once he came toward her in the night but heard a splash and found there was nobody on deck and no sign in the water except for a shiny wake, where maybe some sea beast was ripping through the waves. Once a sailor in the crow's nest saw a mermaid, her tail all diamonds like a snow figure in sunshine.

"Then for a long time there was peace, and the captain seemed to give over worrying and be peart.

"But one morning he wasn't in his cabin—wasn't anywhere that they could discern. And afterward the first mate took charge, and he made sure the sailors went aloft by twos, and he asked the passengers to hunker belowdecks until they were called to promenade in the air or wash their clothes or do whatever they needed."

Ingledove remembered the young woman's face, her narrow shining gown, her tiny features. She shivered, the drug flowing cold through her veins.

"That's a booger story, ain't it? Enough to give you the all-overs. You'll be better soon—I'll tote you until we get to the last turning of the stairs. Then you'll have no trouble scampering barefoot the last whorl of the way. And the Witchmaster will know what ails your brother." Knox Messer stood, stamping his feet and swinging his arms, scanning the nearby mountainsides.

"What happened? What happened on the ship?"

The young Witchmaster frowned, as if reluctant to finish— perhaps he now felt that it had been ill advised to tell such a tale. "For a while, nothing. As they neared the coast one night after moonrise, the mate felt something amiss. He climbed to the deck and saw the wheel spinning—the sailors who'd been on watch had vanished, and a great white snake was wrapped around the mainmast, basking in the starlight. After that the people took to currachs and abandoned the ship, which got wave-throwed on the shoals near Hatteras, and the mate died when it foundered, and most who'd gone in the ship's boats were sopped and drowned in rough waters, coming ashore."

"What was it?"

"I don't know. They say that there were huge spiral markings in the sands the next day." He gazed about uneasily and added, "Later on, a big shed snakeskin was found in the wreckage, coiled around the mast."

THE WINDING STAIR

"This is it—the last turning," Knox declared, helping Ingledove slide from his shoulders.

"There must've been bravery in that tonic. I never saw the world from so high up." She shook out her skirts and took the rucksack from him. He had carried her and the pack and his own poke for an hour. Now mist and dusk were beginning to blur the edges of the trees, so that the landscape seemed smoky.

"You're but a slip of a maid. That's what my grandmarm would say." He jerked his head toward Lang, who had halted some twenty feet back, listening. "You hear?"

She held still, her hand on the boy's sleeve.

"Yes," she said finally.

"I been heeding it for thirty minutes or more," he told her. "And watching him—your brother heard it long before I did. I saw him working his head around, trying to find out where it was from. He was startled at first, but now he's cinched tight. Like he's traipsing in a dream—see there?"

She stared at Lang. He did look entranced, leaning against a tree, his expression slack and his eyes half-closed. He wasn't paying any attention to what they were saying. The wild sweet singing came from miles away, swirling through the coves, dashing against the heights—as if it was seeking something through the distance. When it swelled, she felt a sharp panic.

"We've got to get him up there." She looked about, surprised to see that there was no more path; they had come to a ledge overhanging a steep drop.

"You'll run better light and bare," Knox said. "It's tender on sore feet. I'd just slow you; I'm really too big for the staircase. There's a part where I have to crawl. Even then I'm squeezed."

"Well, thank you," she said, still unsure what he meant for them to do.

He hoisted her by the waist, planting her feet on a shelving of stone. "See that branch of laurel, the one that's wiggled-and-wingled? Pull it toward you."

She did as he told her, drawing the twisted bough forward until she could see an opening in the dense shrubbery.

"Now jump through there like a mouse, and keep climbing on the path until you pop out. It's not far, no more than twenty minutes. I'll heave your brother after. And I'll stay until the time's gone past. If the way seems narrow, keep going. Some call it the Witchmaster's stovepipe."

Leaning forward, she touched his fingertips.

"Knox Messer, I won't forget this—I'm glad we found you. We might've died—"

"No, no, not that. You'll be fine. Him too, someday." The boy nodded. "Go on, while you can still see."

"What about you?"

"Don't worry about me. We passed a place where one of my cousins roosts, not half a mile ago."

"I didn't—"

"No, you're not meant to see. Go on."

Ducking under the tangled limbs of rhododendron, she crouched low, the pack wobbling and boots knocking against her side. In a few moments the space opened, and she could stand, letting her eyes get used to the gloom inside the bushes.

Lang's shape blotted much of the daylight behind her as, bent low, he wormed through after her.

"This is—fun," he said.

Suddenly Ingledove remembered how Malia had slipped into the laurel hell near Sally's clearing and disappeared.

"Come on, then." Kneeling, she brushed her hand across the soft carpet. "It's mossy steps. With stone risers."

"So strange." His voice sounded pleased.

The matted stair twisted through the laurel, gyring in a manner that seemed nigh impossible. They were now scaling a cleft in the rock, ingeniously carved into a staircase. The girl reminded herself that Knox had been here often enough, so the climb must be safe. It was like mounting the spiral ladder of a lighthouse, only underground, with the stairs fastened to the walls instead of shooting up the center. She kept corkscrewing, the moss damp and cool on her feet. Through limbs high above, she caught glimpses of sky and a cloud like another mountain towering above the fissure.

"Lang." She turned because she couldn't sense him any longer. "Lang, where are you?"

"Right behind you," he replied. Soon he came around the curve and bumped into her. "I was just listening. I heard— some bird, I think it was. Can there be nightingales in the South?"

She felt a weight of weariness. "Mockingbirds, Lang. It must have been a mockingbird."

He was silent and still, his hand fumbling for her arm in the dim light. She could hear a tendril of the soprano voice groping to find them, like a wisp of smoke rising in the Witchmaster's chimney. Lacing her fingers with her brother's, she tugged him lightly, and he followed. It felt sweet but sad to her, to be leading him in such a way, as if he were the younger one. She meant to save him—him with his glisten-ing black wound in the twilight of the laurel hell. The stair seemed to have tired him, so that he moved slowly.

The irregular branches with their down-hanging leaves grew sparser, and more sunlight seeped through. But now they had to use hands and feet to clamber upward.

"Oh!" Ingledove tripped and tumbled on the tussocks of moss at the wide upper landing. Laughing, she reached to help Lang out, but her voice caught as she glimpsed the windings below, funneling into the dark.

"I'd hate to go the way we came," he observed, kneeling on the moss.

"Then we'll have to fly. You know, I don't see how Knox ever made it through there." Brushing twigs and leaves from a skirt streaked with green, she surveyed her brother. "You look a sight," she told him; "your face is smeared with dirt."

"You look a sight worse," he returned, grinning at her. She smiled, comforted. "That braid's all sticks and leaves."

She felt it and burst out laughing. "You'd be as bad if you'd been riding a giant through the treetops."

The two searched across the slope, not seeing anything resembling a place of shelter. Approaching dusk had flung three or four stars into the sky as harbingers of the night to come, but the high, slanting ground was still lit by final rays of sunlight. A mist rolled over the mountainside, welcome to their sweaty faces. As they neared the crest, Ingledove pointed to a stunted mountain ash growing in a circle of velvety moss, its seed heads and the leaves close around them already colored a brilliant persimmon.

"Look there—that's pretty—"

As she spoke, she saw someone standing near the tree, watching their progress. It seemed almost as though he had been waiting for them to arrive. Or for someone else, maybe. As they drew nearer, she saw that he was dressed similarly to her brother but in a more finely woven shirt and sash over loose pants tucked into boots.

He seemed older than Lang, though no more than a year or so. Nineteen at the very most.

"We're hunting for—Knox Messer sent us up the winding stair to find the Master of Witchmasters," she called out.

"I was expecting . . ."

He looked from one to the other and back again. The girl had become a narrow observer of her schoolmates since moving to Asheville; she noted a little twitch at the corner of his mouth, the careless casting away of a twig he had been flexing in his fingers. He struck her as disappointed in something, perhaps that people he had been certain would come had turned out to be only strangers. He also appeared puzzled, she thought, the area between his eyebrows contracting ever so slightly. In one quick searching glance she took in his distress—whatever its source—but resolved that she would pursue him until he led the way to their destination. After all, they would never have gained the path this far without help, for surely they could never have discovered on their own that the curly line on Sally's map meant the stair through the laurel. She thought he would help, that he could be kind, although he wasn't really listening to her. Just like a boy! His face was as alien to her as his clothing had once been. She'd never seen a man with such long hair—black, with a dull sheen, and hanging to his waist in a ponytail. The Adantans were part Cherokee, according to Knox, but this one looked like nobody else she'd ever seen, with his blue eyes bright under flaring brows.

"We need to see the Witchmaster. It's my brother; he's ill. He's been bitten . . ."

She saw that Lang had turned and was again leaning toward the direction of the voice, which sounded diminished and insectlike.

"Where's your sister?" Again the young man gave the impression of being perplexed. Perhaps he had confused her with someone else, a girl with a younger sister. An Adantan, she remembered, like her mother, *a daughter of Adantis.*

"I don't have a sister. There's just me and him. Nobody else." Saying the words made her feel terribly sad and worn, and the strength that the bloodroot tonic had lent now abandoned her as quickly as it had come, so that she wanted only to sit and cry. "Knox Messer led us to the stairs. We've got to see—"

"I'm sorry; I wasn't thinking properly. What's the matter with him?" And suddenly he did seem more interested, and she noticed that his mouth under the straight, sharp nose had a softness at odds with the bold cut of the rest of his face.

"A bite. Right here." She touched herself between the collarbone and the heart.

Going to Lang, he spoke to him in a low voice. Her brother replied listlessly and did not object as the stranger examined his eyes and briefly pulled aside the neck of his shirt.

"It's too dusky to tell much," he remarked.

"Will he see us—will you make the Master of Witchmasters see us?" The girl impetuously seized the sleeve of his shirt. There were tears in her eyes that it was now too dark to see, but they seemed to have crept into her voice as well, adding a note of mournful pleading to her words.

The young man appeared startled; he stopped and stared at her face, looking even more bewildered than before.

"There's mystery here . . ." He fell silent but took her hand from his arm and pressed it. "Yes," he promised, giving a little quirk of a smile, "I will make him see you and do whatever he can. Though you're not quite one of us, are you? You're not Adantan, so how you met Knox Messer and how you come to wear the clothes you wear, I don't fathom. Letting in outlanders is against our ways. But it's too late, and you're already in, and you need help." He seemed to have made up his mind while speaking, and, at least for the moment, to have shrugged off the disappointment that he had felt on first seeing them.

While they spoke, the clouds and light had changed, and

the sunset had transformed a mackerel sky into long rose-colored fields, reminders of some faraway flatlands—plowed meadows of dreams, heaped with roses.

"Our mother—Marm was Adantan," she began, explaining hurriedly as the bright clouds began to fade.

Meanwhile the boy—she could hardly decide whether to call him a boy or a man—coaxed Lang forward. But after a minute he simply picked him up in his arms and carried him like a baby. She couldn't imagine that her brother would accept such a thing, but he did, his head lying against the other's shoulder, his eyes closed in exhaustion.

"It's all right," the young man told her. "He's done in. Stay right with me, or you'll get lost."

After that she clung close as a burr, determined not to drop behind. It wasn't long until they came to a bank of moss in the woods, a spot no doubt deep in shade even at noonday. There, passing through a veil of vines and standing in pitchy dark, Ingledove watched as a streak of phosphorescence showed a wooden door with iron hinges and a knocker like a crowned serpent, glinting above glowing smudges.

"What's that?"

"Just a little natural magic. Some luminous mold."

The door, swollen with summer heat and humidity, budged with difficulty. Then she stood blinking in the doorway as Lang was borne inside.

"Come in, and close—"

The voice was cut off, as if removed to a second more-distant room. She stepped over the threshold and leaned against the heavy door to push it shut.

Looking around, she realized that she must be too weary to

be surprised by anything. Because beyond the rude door was a chamber that showed the mark of generations of people, with their own interests, where nothing had ever been thrown away. There was a satisfying impression of layers of time and sensibility in the objects once cherished: ornate Victorian cases displaying eggs and feathers and hummingbird nests; Windsor chairs and benches with bulbous turnings, worn satiny smooth; a stack of blankets that resembled braided sashes, each dyed in the colors of Indian corn; several oil paintings of fairies—a pair of winged lovers in a bird's nest, the picture surrounded by a frame cunningly whittled to mimic twigs, and a shimmery depiction of fairies sparkling as they chased a fox across the snow—and one of a child holding a hawthorn branch in bloom; a pair of dulcimers curiously carved with the heads of ravens and tails of serpents; an old wooden daybed heaped with embroidered pillows; a cabinet of Tiffany vases and saltcellars; a frame containing foxed slips of paper which upon inspection proved to be receipts for small-clothes orders signed by Presidents Andrew Jackson and James Knox Polk and someone named Wilusdi Thomas.

For a moment she forgot everything else and moved around the parlor, taking all in. Pausing at a chest-on-chest containing hundreds of drawers, she ran her fingers over them and pulled one open. Within lay a jumble of objects: a moss agate; a silver ring set with a star sapphire; a quartz arrow point. Leaning against the heavy case was a silver-footed staff; the color of honey, it was silky from long handling, the tangle of carvings at the top gone blurred and unrecognizable. But the focal point of the room was a round maple table, boldly tigered in grain, with legs like great cat feet that gripped iridescent globes. Centered on it was something mysterious, veiled by a shawl of hand-tatted lace in a design made up of thousands and thousands of white flowers. Whatever was beneath shifted like water and threw off refracted colors—she could see them trembling under the lace blossoms. She put out her hand to touch the hidden thing.

"Down here!"

The young man called, and, drawing back, she crossed the room and peered into a narrow hallway, lit by an occasional sconce.

"You have electricity . . ."

"Not very modern. Knob and tube. It's good so long as the chipmunks don't gnaw into the walls. And there's a generator."

"Where are you?"

"Keep coming—here I am." He leaned from a door, nodded at her, and disappeared once more.

Following, she stepped over the sill. Lang was lying on a high curtained bed, bare to the waist. She could see the wound glowing like a black star on his chest. Drawn close to a stepstool and piled blankets was a table scattered with bottles and saucers, a bowl of water, a mortar and pestle, and some sharp instruments in a tumbler of alcohol.

"I put him here because I'd started a fire earlier to burn the mustiness from the room. I'd been expecting—a guest. But I must have been mistaken."

"What's happened to him?" The girl stared at the injury, which now showed a narrow slit where there had been a swelling.

"It's already lanced, cleaned." He nodded toward the

hearth. "You didn't mind skipping that part, I guess. The cloth's burning in the fire."

The rags in the flames were scribbled with deep blue matter. She looked at them and shivered.

"What's the matter with your feet?"

"It's just blisters. But they're bad. Knox Messer put on some ointment and gave me Jarrett's Special—"

"That's fine, then, for now."

"And where has he gone?"

"Your brother? He's not unconscious, if that's what you mean. He's only sleeping. We'll have to wake him to finish the rest of the treatment."

"No, I mean the *Witchmaster*." She stared at him, a thought glimmering just out of reach. Wouldn't the Master of Witchmasters be ancient, with a knotty cane and a silvery beard that reached to his knees? She had pictured a tame enchanter, with robes and a wand tucked in his sleeve and a wise grandfatherly manner—someone who would always arrive in the nick of time and set the mayhem of the mountains aright, returning them with a *poof!* to Danagasta.

"He's here—he's me. I'm the Master."

Ingledove kept on staring at him, neither denying nor accepting what he had said, though she felt more weary than before, knowing that there was no wand, no grandfather, no *poof!* at all. She wanted to laugh, but she had gone too far beyond exhaustion to find even a note of hysteria.

"Somehow I thought there'd be a really old, old man," she said at last.

"Sorry to disappoint," he said, giving her an amused glance

as he began putting stoppers in his array of bottles. "There was one before, and there'll be one again, if I'm lucky."

"It's not that. It's that I—well, I imagined a wizard who'd wave a wand and send us home, just like that! I didn't know what a witchmaster was. I guess I still don't." She sighed, suddenly wanting nothing but sleep.

"Wands are for outlanders—for stage magicians—though dowsing sticks are a kind of wand for finding water." He began arranging the bottles on a salver.

"Knox Messer had one of those," she whispered, wondering whether he was now annoyed with her.

"Wizards and witches aren't playthings to Adantans—I'm a witch*master*, not a witch. Make sense? There's always one of us who's chosen to spend childhood the way I did, memorizing and studying with the current Master, being sent across the ocean for an apprenticeship there. There's not anything jolly about it, nothing anybody would want if he knew the cost, right at the start. The Master is a servant bound to all of Adantis, but he's set apart. He has a knowledge that makes him different. Our people are a joy-loving tribe, but often he is forced to be dead serious. Our people are storytellers and lovers of traipsing the mountains, but he spends his boyhood mured up in libraries. Or girlhood—the Master is as likely to be female as male." He paused, frowning at the assembled powders on the tray. "I don't know why I told you all that—it must be because you're not quite Adantan. Though of course you are, through your mother.

"Did you hear someone singing when you were outside?" He spoke with force, and he still wasn't looking at her; he was bending, examining the wound. Perhaps he was only pretending, perhaps he did not want to meet her eyes.

"Malia," she whispered.

"You'll have to tell me about what happened, you know. In the morning. About whether you met somebody in the mountains."

She yawned and nodded. "Yes, I will. And we did."

"Maybe you'd like to sleep on the trundle bed. I've always thought this room pretty, and it's meant to be a girl's special retreat. It once belonged to a witchmaster's daughter, but no one has slept in it for years."

She thanked him, feeling that she couldn't possibly change her clothes or do anything more than drop onto the child's trundle that he had pulled from under the bed. The sheets on it were dusty. She didn't mind, couldn't possibly care, and had never been so dirty in her life.

"Here, you'll need to help me with your brother first. I want to give him a draught of medicine. It's a tonic and painkiller and sleeping pill rolled into one. Then he can sleep through the night and let his body knit itself back together." Taking a cup from the nearby dresser, he carried it to the bed and lifted Lang into a sitting position. "He must have been drained, because he fell asleep instantly. Call him, and see if you can wake him."

"Lang, Lang," she coaxed, petting him on the cheek.

The injured patient moaned slightly, his eyelids lifting until she could see the whites of his eyes. Repeatedly he tried to speak, the syllables of her name wallowing incoherently in his mouth.

"Lang . . ."

He surfaced enough to drink, though half the contents splashed across the bedding.

"What was he saying?" With a few quick strokes, the Witchmaster wiped the remains of the spilled drink from the boy's face.

"Ingledove."

"Ingledove? What do you know about that name?" The Witchmaster's face had changed, so that the girl felt frightened and suddenly wakeful and alert. She was sure that he was shocked and perhaps angry, and his intent blue eyes seemed to demand what she could not understand.

She put up a hand, as if to ward off a blow.

"I've scared you," he said immediately. "It's just that—" He stopped mid-sentence.

"*I'm* Ingledove. It's me."

His mouth was slightly open. Abruptly he slapped his forehead once, twice, three times and began to laugh. Tears came into his eyes, but he still laughed the more.

"Stop it, stop it, stop it," she whispered, gripping the bedpost in both hands. When he did not halt, she went to him and seized his arm, staring into his face until he returned her gaze and ceased as suddenly as he had begun. She felt for the first time that there was a kind of power in him, because it was as if she had gripped on to a live wire, the electricity from which surged from her very heels to her head and made her hair stand up.

"I'm sorry," he said, his eyes fixed on hers. "It's just that it's proving much harder being the Master than I'd realized." Taking her hand, he led her from the bedroom, first glancing at Lang, who had already fallen back into deep sleep.

She hurried beside him, looking at his set face by the yellow light of the sconces. In the front room he went straight to the table and fingered a corner of the shawl as if he might jerk it away. Under the lace flowers could be seen a swirl of color, then a shimmering of white. She felt an intense desire to know what moved underneath.

"No," he said, relinquishing the corner of delicate cloth and letting it fall to the polished table. "Not now. Here, let me show you something else." He crossed to the chest of tiny drawers, and Ingledove noticed with a flicker of alarm that she had not closed the one explored in idle curiosity. "You count over, by the number of the month, like so," he said, his finger skimming across the surface. "Then down for the number of the date.

"Here it is." He tapped his finger on a knob. "The one I'd set aside for today. Open it."

She slid out the drawer. Inside, next to a pressed sprig of meadow rue, an emerald mounted on a gold band, and an eaglet's downy feather, was a strip of handmade paper, a creamy coarse stock flecked with moss. On it, in violet ink, with flourishes, was the single word *Ingledove*.

MASTER OF WITCHMASTERS

"You outlanders reveal your names too easily," the Master was saying; "They give dark things power over you."

Ingledove closed her eyes. Though she still wanted to know how he had learned her name, she was feeling clean and almost contented, knowing that they'd been lost and in danger but were now found and safe from harm, at least temporarily. On waking, she had stared at Lang, who was asleep with both arms flung out and the black star still glistening on his chest. Then she had taken a bath, dumping fragrant oil into the tub. Though her bandages had to be soaked and then tugged away, and her heels had smarted when she had climbed in, she hadn't cared. She had lolled and let the soap bubbles climb to the rounded lip: delicious! Every now and then she had added more piping-hot water from a canister on the wall, but the cast-iron tub held the heat for a long time. She had washed and rinsed her hair three times until she smelled like a gardenia. Afterward she had followed her nose down a narrow set of stairs to the kitchen, where she had eaten a breakfast of ham and oatcakes and eggs, served by the impossibly small cook. The old lady called herself Dessie, and though she might have been pretty once, she now had the face of a butternut-head mountain doll, with lined cheeks, skin the color of coffee-and-milk, and a nose that brought her whole face to a point. She looked even more diminutive because of her hunched spine, disguised under a woven shawl. The girl had been sorry when Dessie had finished the dishes and darted into the pantry. When she had gone searching, she had found the cook flown, but later on she had reappeared as laundrywoman, carrying the clothes from the rucksacks, the white linen now clean and almost stainless, folded neatly.

"What?" Ingledove jerked to attention, opening her eyes and turning to face the Witchmaster. He was thumbing through a leather-bound book, scanning the pages for a reference.

"Does that woman, the one you called Malia—does she know your brother's name?"

"Yes, I think so. They were whispering together in the yard. When she left, he told me her name."

"He told you what she chose for him to know. I'm sure she guards her own identity, her own names." He gave a single nod and picked up the volume, settling himself to read on a humpbacked couch. "Such beings are cut off from all else on earth and beyond. And that acts like a black seed. In time, it sprouts and flourishes and draws dark elements of the air and forest to sit on its branches. You see? At first the kernel is just a shadow and an emptiness, but later on it takes shape and grows and blots out the sun."

"Even trees have names—do you know who or what she is?" It occurred to her that the Witchmaster of Adantis might have more than names that he chose to keep private.

"I have some ideas. That's what I'm working on. But I'd like to see her before I say."

She wrinkled her nose. "I'd just as soon never meet up with her ever again."

"There are ways to see without being seen," he began, his attention alighting on the drape of white flowers on the cat-footed table.

Ingledove noticed and wondered what he meant. She didn't want to ask; she did not like his evasiveness.

"Do we have to call you Master?"

"You can call me Jarrett. A witchmaster has to be careful not to reveal his names, but that one will do. I'm distantly re-lated to Chief Nimrod Jarrett Smith: a good man who could keep a secret and was always welcome in our houses. That's his picture over there—"

The daguerreotype showed a curly-haired man with a square face. To Ingledove he didn't look Cherokee except for the long hair, but he had been a chief all the same.

"—and I have his presentation sword. He was a sergeant in Will Thomas's Company B. Thomas was also Chief, a Welsh-man but adopted as son by a Cherokee chief, and an impor-tant figure to the Eastern Band—"

"Have you ever used it?" She knew nothing about the East-ern Band, but she was curious about the sword.

"I've had occasion, once or twice or so. It's quite sharp and has been tempered and blessed by witchmasters."

The young man scanned the pages before him without giving any sign of what he was feeling. Nor, she felt sure, would he explain why or exactly how many times he had used Chief Nimrod Jarrett Smith's sword. He was dressed less formally than the day before—his coarse shirt had no sash, and he wore close-fitting leather pants like Lang's, one leg showing the scars of rip and repair.

She mulled over his words. "You said," she began hesitantly, "that there are different ways of seeing."

He lifted his face from the book and looked at her, his eyes not meeting hers but examining her features, her unloosed hair, the linen dress snug to her slim figure.

"I could try," he said in a low voice, as if not speaking to her; "I haven't had much success at it lately, but maybe now that you're here and things are as they are, I won't have so much trouble with interruptions . . . I don't have any reason to wait and hope anymore. So I won't be distracted. I can clear my mind and focus on seeing this Malia."

He marked the page with a slip of paper and stood. "You may as well come close, then."

She drew near to the table where the Witchmaster paused, his hand on the veil.

"This is one of the greatest treasures of Adantis. It was inherited by the first Master, who was one-half Cherokee and received the gift from an uncle. It had been passed down for many generations. Originally it came from the forehead of an Uktena. The hunter was gored in the attempt to win it and never got over the gash, or so the story is told."

She hadn't understood his remarks and didn't know what an Uktena might be, but she kept her mouth shut. She wanted to find out what was under the cloth.

Jarrett stared at the wisp of lace in his fingers. She wondered whether he felt reluctant to show what lay beneath.

"This is the Ulunsuti, and there's nothing else like it." The lace began slipping along the table, tugged by his hand. He paused, indecisive, and when he spoke there was an undercurrent of bitterness in his voice. "I've rarely revealed it to anybody. I don't know why I'm sharing it with a little girl."

"I stopped being one of those a long time ago," Ingledove declared, displaying a spark of indignation as she straightened to full height. She was no child. In fact, she had been prevented from prolonging her childhood by the loss of too many things: a wanderlust father with dreams of fortune; a house made from wide maple boards next to the silver tresses of a mountain stream; Marm, who was always laboring in the kitchen or garden but loved the wildflowers and birds by day and the splendor of the stars by night—and was all the time something unknown and secret, a daughter of Adantis. Then she'd lost a whole world—of drowned or burned towns along Hazel Creek, with mill and mine, church and school. She knew what it was to feel abandoned by everything but ghosts. Had Marm ever felt the same way, after leaving home for the sake of a man? Fleetingly she saw that she and Marm were the same, except that her mother had been able to replace Adantis with Hazel Creek, which was also a secret, isolated realm— and she? what could she make her Adantis? her Hazel Creek? For she had never felt at home in Asheville, even with Danagasta and her brother there. No, she was not a child, and already she would appear a stranger to her own mother, for she had left the little girl's body behind.

The Witchmaster smiled at her, and his eyes were startling in the fair, strong-boned face. The Irish in him, she guessed—the contrast between black hair and blue eyes.

"You're right. And I'm sorry," he said; "perhaps I just wished you closer to my own age."

"The Ulunsuti," she prompted.

"Yes," he said. "Well, this is what Mooney says about the stone: 'Whoever owns the Ulunsuti is sure of success in hunting, love, rainmaking, and every other business, but its great use in life is prophecy.'" During this recital, Jarrett had let his eyelids drift shut. When he paused, they opened again with a bold flash of blue like a jay streaking past a window. He continued: "'When it is consulted for this purpose, the future is seen mirrored in the clear crystal as a tree is reflected in the quiet stream below, and the conjurer knows whether the sick man will recover, whether the warrior will return from battle, or whether the youth will live to be old.' So Mooney says."

"Lang." She trembled in a breeze from the door, propped ajar with a chunk of sapphire. The chance of finding out whether her brother would live seemed terrible—the possibility of being certain of his death so much worse than not knowing, seesawing between hope and fear.

"Yes, the Ulunsuti can tell us if he'll live—if it will. But what is more to our purpose is catching a glimpse of this Malia. And from seeing her we may learn more about Lang's fate."

Ingledove remembered her father, perhaps dead, perhaps

alive. Could she see him again—the careless blond man who thought so highly of himself, who rushed from one money-making scheme to another? Maybe he would be seated under a banana tree by an azure bay, with green and rose parrots on an arm and a white hat shading his eyes. He might be a rich plantation owner, with servants ferrying drink after drink to his chair. Maybe he had replaced his own with another family. Or maybe he had failed and was penniless, flotsam caught at the edge of the Amazon, unable to come home. No. She did not believe that any witchmaster's magic could show his face. She had no hope that something kept under wraps on a peculiar round table could help them in any way.

"You're just so lucky, aren't you? You can make it rain, and you have good fortune in love and hunting."

"An ironic tone doesn't suit you," the Master said absently, his eyes on the wobbling patches of color, barely seen through the lace.

When Jarrett again swept the shawl toward him, the thin web of flowers trickled from the Ulunsuti like snow. The exposed crystal blazed, its clarity shot through by sparkling veins. It reminded the girl of nothing so much as a gigantic diamond, cut to shine prismatic in light. It was not a single gem but three, fused into one, with many smaller projections clustering around the outer edges.

"What's that, in the center?" Ingledove was impressed despite herself—she'd never seen anything like this living rock.

"The reddish line? It's a kind of vein." Flicking a finger over a sharp edge of the crystal, he lifted his hand and let a drop splash onto the surface. He pressed the cut and let more blood flow. The fissure in the mineral brightened, going from rust to red.

"Why did you—"

"The Ulunsuti has been fed every seven days for hundreds of years. The Tellers say that the Uktena will rise and destroy the owner of the stone if it is not fed. I don't know if that's true. But it's enough for me that it has been sated for so long. Every Witchmaster has valued tradition. And even before Adantis came to be, the stone was hungry."

He pinched the incision, as he must have done many times before. "Maybe you think the blood offering is barbaric. I didn't like it much when I first saw the Witchmaster nicking a fingertip every week. But now I like the idea that it's something every Master has done, and before that a line of Cherokee, when the world was wild. I like it that our blood is mingled together in the transparent heart. And I don't know that I believe that an Uktena would come rampaging over the mountains to devour me, but maybe something would happen that I didn't like, if I broke that chain. Because in some sense the Ulunsuti is still alive."

"Look—there are more flecks." She watched the scraps of color flickering inside the crystal.

"That's the image forming. Not everybody can make it out."

"It's like reflections rocking on a stream—or no, not on the surface but inside, deep in the water."

Briefly the Master returned her glance, his expression unreadable.

"There she is!" Ingledove cried out, having for an instant seen a female face before it fell apart into waves.

"I wasn't paying attention." Jarrett let his eyes close. She imagined that he must be concentrating his thoughts. However it was, he regained the unfamiliarity he had worn under the mountain ash tree.

When she checked the stone, the motes were again coming together, and for an instant she saw the Witchmaster with—but was it Malia? As she stared, a swell buoyed the image, and it trembled and exploded into specks.

"I'm not sure that was she. I don't think so."

He didn't reply, and his eyes were still veiled as the colors wavered together, forming anew. When he at last opened them, the stray atoms were being drawn to a spot deep in the mineral, and for a few instants both could clearly see him with a light-haired woman, not Malia.

"She's pretty, but she isn't Malia. She seems familiar." Her voice had sunk to a whisper. The picture was failing now, as if whipped by the wind, although from time to time she caught glimpses of one or both, their heads close together.

She was surprised when Jarrett laughed.

"Well, she should be." He looked rueful, gathering the shawl as if to cover the crystal again.

"Don't! It looks so strange."

To her surprise, he was disconcerted, a blush tinging his cheeks. "I thought they'd be gone now. I wanted to see Malia; I wanted to see Lang. Maybe that's part of the problem, that I tried to envision a man and a woman. It's my fault; there's a link between the Master and the Ulunsuti, and it keeps showing me—I'll need to clear my mind."

"What did you mean, *she should be*?" She hadn't been listening; she was still puzzling over what he had meant. Did the

Ulunsuti show past as well as future? For she had seen some-thing of Marm in the face. It had startled; it had given her an extraordinary flash of longing—a hurt to the heart weirdly mingled with the joy of recognition.

When she looked at him, Ingledove thought that he, too, seemed disturbed.

"It's lonely here, being the Master," he began; "I was expect-ing someone my own age. That's what the stone showed me. But then you and Lang arrived. And you're not grown. You hardly even know who you are, or what you can do, or what your gifts are."

"Why are you talking about gifts? I don't have—"

"No, everyone has gifts." He touched her shoulder briefly before drawing away. "We say that gifts come from the Appor-tioner. That is one of our people's sacred names for the Maker. In Adantis, we believe that there is one people but many gifts. You see? I did not know my gifts once. When I discovered them, I was handed over to the Witchmaster, and I spent years memorizing the lore of the Adantans and the beliefs and even the errors of the Old and New worlds."

"I don't know what you mean about gifts—"

"They will come," he said simply.

"But what about—if not Malia, who is she?" She saw that the colors were spinning in the rock, whirling as if a vortex had caught and toyed with them. For an instant they reassem-bled, and Ingledove saw that the two figures were embracing; then the image wobbled and flew apart like a flock of startled butterflies. Turning, she saw that the Master's gaze rested on the wall opposite.

"Will it keep making pictures?"

"What? The Ulunsuti—yes, the fragments will keep dancing and refracting and occasionally meeting."

"But you haven't told me what they mean."

"Well, I think the time is some years away, maybe five or six. Maybe seven. You see, I thought it was soon, but I was wrong. Such things can be pretty hard to tell."

"I still don't know what you're saying," she cried out, feeling frustrated. "What use is it? At first I thought it was— Who is it?" They had not seen Malia nor glimpsed a Lang well and strong.

"Don't you know?" The Witchmaster's glance was on a mirror, a long narrow one framed in scalloped wood, crowned with a carved urn of flowers. "There . . ."

Ingledove peered into the speckled glass and found her own face and Jarrett's swimming in its gloom.

"What—" She stopped, her eyes going to the faceted crystal with its kaleidescope of shade and light.

"I only knew the name and the image. It's rare to receive a word from the Ulunsuti, forming in the mind syllable by syllable. The face kept appearing, long before I had the name. After a while I could hardly see anything else, and I thought she would be here any hour."

"And so you were waiting yesterday."

"Yes, I was."

For the first time, Ingledove felt sorry for the Witchmaster as what he meant grew plain. The thought seemed not astonishing or even embarrassing but simply a pity. Its sadness welled up in her as surely as the bits and ribbons of color had whirled from the center of the Ulunsuti. She had her brother and Danagasta, but he had no one. Once she and Lang arrived, the dream that had been in his mind must have been rent and the picture lost in a flurry of motes. The image was years off, not close enough to touch.

"But is it real?"

"It's something that may happen, if all things go well."

She felt compelled to make him say the words, to be sure. "So that girl, the young woman in the crystal, she is . . ." As if to make sure, she turned toward the table, but there was nothing except a flurry of confetti where the figures had been.

He spoke only the one word: "Ingledove."

BETROTHED

Sge!
Ravens of the cardinal points,
Raven of the North,
Raven of Wahili, Southern mountain,
Raven of the East,
Raven of the West.
Black, Red, Blue, and White—
Birds that compass: hear me!

Black raven, you never fail—
Take this ghost,
This black-starred illness,
This springer-into-being—
Bury it in lonely crevices
Of Sanigilagi, high mountain.

Let it sleep forever
In the darkening land.

Sge!
Red raven, strong adawehi,
Draw close and hear—
Pluck out this worm
Of poisonous night—
Plunge it into cracks
Of Whiteside Mountain,
Above the headwaters
Of the Tuckasegee.

Blue raven,
Shining blue-black
On the thrusting currents,
White raven of Wahili,
Southern mountain,
Dazzling as noonday snow—
You black, red, blue, and white
Messengers of the Giver,
Restore this man to wholeness.

Ingledove watched as Jarrett burned dried blossoms of wild
parsnip and tobacco and lobelia on a brazier. He revealed only
that they were "efficacious against witches and wizards,"
though he did not think Malia to be either. Now he sat cross-
legged on the floor by the bed where Lang slept restlessly,
hands twitching on the coverlet. What the Master was doing

was mysterious to her, though earlier he had said prayers that seemed familiar—but before that he had peeled and sharpened holly sticks and hammered them at the corners of the door tucked into the mountain's slope. They were, he told her, another traditional defense against black magic. He seemed to put a lot of store in handed-down remedies. His chant was a version of an old sacred formula of the Cherokee. She thought that the Giver must be another sacred name, and she speculated that the birds joined as one were an image of unity, perhaps even of health.

Already she had given over thinking about the earlier mystery—the revelation of the Ulunsuti. It was impossible to accept and too big to reject without a struggle and as strange as anything that had happened since they had left the Copper Baron's house. Although now and then she was surprised into remembering by the sudden flash of blue eyes or the downward tilt of the Witchmaster's profile, reminding her of the angle of his face as seen in the stone, she managed to put those moments aside—to be thought about at some later time when Lang did not need her attention. It seemed that, without a word uttered, she and Jarrett had agreed not to speak of the prophetic stone. What was some visionary, perhaps possible future as opposed to her brother's life-and-death wrestle with the venom in his body?

"He's better; it's good that he has slept so long again. He has had three days of rest, gathering strength. He has awakened each evening and proved that he's lucid. All that is fine. And the swelling is gone." Jarrett got to his feet and leaned over Lang's body, gently checking the wound on his chest and adding to the poultice under the clean linen bandage. The lids were not quite closed, and the eyes could be seen, flicking from one side to another as if in alarm.

"But I do wish he weren't so wakeful at night," he added.

"That's when she sings the loudest—is that why?"

"I think that's part of the reason, maybe not all. He's drawn to her, and she's more active in the evenings."

Here the sleeper's eyelids suddenly flew open, and his hazel eyes stared without seeing for a moment before they closed, leaving white crescent moons still showing.

"I don't like the way that—"

"Yes, it was startling. He must be wandering in a dream." The Witchmaster gently slid his hand over Lang's forehead, then swept it across the eyes. The lids closed obediently.

Ingledove flinched; she remembered that same gesture from Hazel Creek, as Danagasta slipped her fingers across Marm's eyelids and closed them for the last time. But her brother wasn't dead. Though moisture stung her eyes, she felt hopeful. He was better; he would get well, and they would walk to the drowned lands and sail across the water in the faded periwinkle boat. She couldn't fathom it wholly—how could they go so far without Malia finding them? And even if she didn't follow them, the fright of possible danger lurking at each crook of the path would be almost unbearable. Perhaps the Witchmaster would see them safe across the reservoir with its underwater ghosts.

"I'm going to see what's happening," he was saying.

"All right," she answered, though she didn't want to leave the safety of this rambling burrow.

Climbing onto the bed, she bent and kissed her brother's cheek. His head jerked slightly, and he spoke. The word sounded like *angel*, so she thought he must have been dreaming of help or else trying to say her name.

It was quiet in the room. Not one note of Malia's song floated so far. She listened before stepping outside, where a sconce threw an hourglass pattern of yellow light on the wall. The front room was empty, the door standing ajar. Tempted, she went to the table, where the white veil was glowing in the dusk. After a moment, she lifted its skein of daisies and peered underneath. The whirlpool of colors fled apart like a school of frightened fish, but just as suddenly resolved into the two figures. They were set close together, and she thought they might be embracing.

"Ingledove!"

With a twitch of the hand, she dropped the cloth, the heat of discovery—had she been caught?—coursing over her body. But no. She was alone. The voice had come from a distance.

Slipping out the half-open door, she stopped in sheer surprise. The wood was glowing, the skin of mold on its surface shimmering with rainbow tints in the light cast from clustered fireflies. They were rising from some luminous tufts close to the sill.

Ducking under the hanging vines, she stepped onto a slope entirely transformed. The thousands of fireflies floating from the earth looked enormous in the humid air, shining like stars as they rose and mingled with the real stars. The girl had seen fireflies before, their bright winks cheering the dark; she had raced to catch them, prisoning them in a canning jar, its top punched with holes. But never had she seen so many in one place. It made her think of the Ulunsuti's veil, as if the white flowers had detached themselves and begun to fly. What further crystalline mystery did they hide under a galaxy of stars?

But the insects were not the only lights. The moss was strewn with smoldering foxfire, the fungi that threaded rotten wood, and here and there she saw scattered jack-o'-lantern mushrooms, partly buried in leaves but emitting a pale orange luminescence. As her eyes became accustomed to the dark, she saw islands of toadstools and mushrooms and ruffles that glowed orange or green or blue or silvery-white. Some were lit only at the base, casting color toward the stalked mushroom above. Most were small, but the clusters of caps and bells and frills made the ground seem a second sky, dotted with softer stars. Gills showed through now-transparent tops of mushrooms, making them into fluted fairy lampshades. The trees were streaked with something luminous as well—bacteria? mold?

A rude pathway meandered between the fungi; she followed its windings until she neared the Witchmaster's stairs through the mountain. There was Jarrett, pounding sharpened wands into picket-fence rings around the chimney top. It looked like nothing so much as the yawning mouth of a great white shark, which she had seen in a book at school, with row after row of serrated teeth visible in the open jaws.

"Here, hold these while I hammer." A strand of hair had fallen across his cheek and clung there. "It's going to weather; I want to finish before the clouds blow in and the storm comes."

Ingledove took the bundle of skewers and handed them to him, one after the other.

"What happened here? It's so bright . . ."

"The fireflies? Yes, they're pretty marvelous tonight. The

magic of luciferin and air, breaking into light—if I were an outlander, I'd study things like that. Though the library here is first-rate," he went on.

"What I meant was the mushrooms and toadstools—like a funny little world of villages with shining domes."

"I should've known; I thought Lampyridae's night garden was amazing when I first came here. I still do. It doesn't come often or when it ought and doesn't make any sense. I don't know half the things that are here. There are *Mycena lux-coeli* from Japan, English glowworms, ghost fungi from Australia, and fire beetles from South America. The garden is jumbled in time and place, though there are some elements that could be local, like faerie fire and honey fungus and false chanterelles."

She handed him a stake, and he thumbed the point at each end, choosing the sharpest to face upward.

"There was a master here who didn't go only to Europe to learn, as all of us do during our apprenticeship. She traveled to Africa and Asia and the Pacific islands, where the girls wear luminous fungi in their hair for ornaments, and a hundred other places, and it was said that her travels around the world made her not only a great master but a witch as well. Lampyridae used her powers for Adantis, but she was a mortal woman and in the end was tempted and destroyed by a demon who took the shape of a man. Not just any man, either. From the ends of his hair to his toes he had a subtle, changeable glowworm shine, and it's said that when they touched each other, the spirit being would deepen in color and seem to pulsate, as if rainbows were struggling beneath his skin. She must have known what he was but have been unable to resist. She was the Master for only a few years and left the next one unready and poorly trained; after her death it was a bad time in Adantis."

Ingledove listened to the story without speaking. During the last three days she had begun believing in what the Witch-master had to say, and though she occasionally wondered if she were falling into a shared madness, she had seen too many odd things not to believe that Adantis was a region made separate by more than miles.

"And she made the garden?"

Jarrett wiped his forehead on the rolled-up sleeve of his shirt and raked tendrils of loose hair from his face before he accepted another stick.

"Yes. She had a love for such things, for gardening and for bioluminescence in its various forms. She collected and studied samples everywhere she traveled. But the garden is not entirely real. No plot could mix such things in one climate and last long. And it's not even fall, so few of the fungi would be visible—the fruiting bodies of many of the mushrooms and toadstools would not yet have appeared. It's enchanted, made to burn more vividly as danger approaches."

Glimpsing the chasm underfoot, Ingledove swayed in sudden vertigo. She had an impulse to press her palms against the soil, but she rejected it and offered him another stick. "Is this as fiery as the fungi get?"

"Yes, I think so. At least, I've never seen the ridge brighter than this. When Adantis is peaceful, there's barely a smudge of light. I first started seeing a blur in the late evenings about three weeks ago. Then the fire beetles and glowworms and fireflies arrived, and the moss became lush and moist."

"What happens in the winter?" Nervous at the thought of

danger, the girl looked over her shoulder but could see nothing except the smears of light on tree trunks and the fungi, glowing like Japanese lanterns for a party.

Taking out a knife, Jarrett sharpened the wands blunted by his mallet.

"In snow the fungi are the most astonishing—I should be used to them, but I still find it wondrous. The cold fire melts the crystals around the mushrooms, so they seem set in the snow like jewels. The beetles trundle about in the flakes. And the summer fireflies come shooting out of the drifts. As the snowflakes go sliding down, the insects flare and waver up through them."

"See those toadstools? I think they're sweet. They look fluted, like lampshades of folded paper." She gestured, her arm gleaming.

"Oh, the bell-shaped ones. They're favorites of mine because of the funny name—*Mycena tintinnabulum.*"

"You like the garden; why was it wrong for her?"

The Witchmaster surveyed the barbs around the maw of the stairs and knotted together a few leftover wands.

"*Ku!* That looks about perfect." He squatted to examine the barrier more closely. "Why was it wrong? I haven't thought that one out," he admitted. "Well, it wasn't wrong to protect Adantis, but it was wrong to alter nature for a private obsession. There are times when the Master skirts the edge of what is forbidden. I've gone over the line before, and I've fasted and repented, as is our way. See, a witchmaster must know what a wizard knows but refrain from dabbling in sorcery. And it was wrong to use magic for nothing but easy pleasure, to follow where that path led without turning away—until it led her into the mandibles of death." He waved his arm over the close-set teeth, as if to emphasize the last phrase. "Maybe she was lured by love of her abilities. I don't know. But human beings weren't meant to create without effort, without humility, without knowing that they can bring art and knowledge into the world only by striving and laboring after what's beautiful and true. The ancient Greeks would have said Lampyridae was guilty of pride."

Although he kept on explaining, Ingledove wasn't taking in the words anymore. She could detect something, a sound worming into her thoughts, becoming louder. Then he fell silent, and she could hear more clearly. Its restlessness seemed to arise from no place in particular, as if it might be a cosmic disturbance, twisting through the swollen, humid stars.

"You heard it?" Jarrett stood, brushing dirt and leaves from his pants. "I've been harkening to that all day."

The girl strained to discover its meaning, shutting her eyes, standing motionless. "It's a kind of slithering," she whispered.

"Ever seen a cottonmouth lying on a rock in the sun, his jaws flopped open so that you can see the white lips and the fangs?" He gazed at the pitchy mouth of the stairs and the pale skewers, sharp and erect. "Set a snake to catch a snake," he said softly.

"Oh. It's a snake you're after . . ."

"Not really. Well, maybe a kind of serpent. Come on, let's go back." Jarrett winced and dropped the tied wands. He held out his palm, where a red mark showed. "They're piercing enough, I guess."

The two climbed the slope, pausing next to a green isle of toadstools, whose caps were set at every angle. The fireflies kept filtering from the moss, constant as a steady rainfall but luminous and upside down.

"I shouldn't blame Lampyridae for what happened, even though a terrible ten years in Adantis followed. Master after Master died, unprepared, swamped by darkness." The Witchmaster was musing, his eyes passing from raft to raft of blue and green, floating in the dark. "I've never been tempted in such a way, though I've dreamed of irresistible—"

"But the garden's so strange and lovely," Ingledove broke in, the surprise she had felt earlier returning in a wave of delight as they passed through the beds of fungi.

"You're right. Such things please the heart. Perhaps it's like some Irish hermit in a beehive hut who happens to see a fairy perched on a Dingle hedgerow—he knows it has no soul and can be cruel as frost, but he can't help feeling lucky and joyful, just the same." He sighed, cocking his head to stare at the lucifer fires of the insects, dashed against the stars. "Or maybe I don't know anything much," he added.

She was listening to the rustling noise again. It was louder than before. "What did you mean about the snake?"

He took her hand and squeezed her fingers lightly. "Long ago, when the border people came across the sea in boats, the world was more uneasy, more haunted. When our ancestors sailed on the ocean, they saw the mermaids floating in phosphorescent algae, they saw birds that swam underwater, they saw bodies like glass that trembled and gleamed, prismatic. These wonders were new to them, fresh and appalling, wilder than their own wild hearts. But in the holds of those ships, there were sometimes stowaways from the Old World, creatures who rejoiced in the wilderness and sought the mountain heights and mingled with the powerful beings of the Cherokee." He paused, setting a firefly on Ingledove's finger like a jewel. "And serpent monsters are famous and feared on both sides of the water."

She lifted her hand, watching the insect stir and flash into the air and lose itself in a crowd of stars.

"I'm not brave, and I'm afraid of pain," she told him. Just then it would have been hard to believe that anything evil could find its way to a spot so entrancing, if not for the distant but tumultuous sound that seemed to threaten something wicked to come.

"There's more in you than you grasp," Jarrett said. "For that matter, there's more to me than I knew a few years back. If it weren't so, you would never have been seen by the Ulunsuti. The stone can show anyone, when asked properly, but it predicts only those who are rare and bold to be a master's companion."

"But I'm not bold," she whispered.

The Witchmaster didn't reply, clambering over rocks beside the orange globes of chanterelles. "There's a mountain story about a boy who was traveling along the Tuckasegee near Cullowhee, years ago when it was known only as a valley of lilies and Adantans freely passed there and made their homes deep in the coves. He met a woman who called herself Amelia, fascinating in manner and appearance, and straightaway he made up his mind to be married. She was a worshipper of Hecate, goddess of ghosts and witchcraft, but he was infatuated by her and excused her—saying to himself that the goddess was only another facet of the Giver. This Amelia threw a big engagement party for him along Caney Fork, and his friends and kin came, and they were dazzled by the grand new house with its fine porches and hallways and rooms filled with precious objects, the like of which had never been seen in Jackson County—and probably still hasn't been seen again, all these many years later.

"The boy's great-granny tottered in, and she saw the lovers and guests sitting down to eat without so much as a by-your-leave or a blessing, and she scolded them then and there. Coming close to the bride-to-be, she examined her with cloudy old eyes that could see better than those of the younger ones at the feast.

" 'You've done et unclean food,' she declared. 'This yere's a monster and no gal.'

"There was a great uproar and hullaballoo, during which the china with its painted gold and silver garlands fluttered away. The bride wept and gnashed her pearly teeth, but in the end she admitted what she was. Suddenly she vanished, and the wide porches and rockers and the fine rooms disappeared with her, and the whole company found itself on the cold ground and went home hungry.

"Some versions of the story say that the old woman was a witchmaster who chased away a fallen angel, and others say that she drove a demon from the boy, and still others conclude that he was possessed by one spirit being and pursued by another. I don't know what it means for your brother, but this is what I fear, when I think of the very worst: that he is already betrothed to evil and death and that there may be no saving him."

Ingledove stood very still, thinking of Marm and the first house on Hazel Creek where she and Lang had been happy and of her brother with the figure who had called herself Malia. Could she appear so close to his age yet be ancient, so delicate yet be potent with evil? The lights danced before her wet eyes, and suddenly she felt faint and hungry. No, she was not bold. The Witchmaster hadn't tried to deny her words, had he? He had only changed the subject. Behind her, the slithering sound increased, became turbulence.

"*Ku!* She must be on the stairs—I thought it was far away—never thought her so near—run! I've got to get—go to the house—"

Stumbling, she ran in a storm of fireflies so dense that she could not see the way, Jarrett dragging at her arm. Once she tripped and lost his hand and fell, landing close to the chill blaze of foxfire and intertwined stems of blue and green mushrooms, the mass of fungi burning away the darkness.

"Hurry, follow me—"

A maelstrom gyred below her, the din pouring like evil smoke from the Witchmaster's chimney. It made a sort of *threshing* noise, she thought. Darting through curtains of light, searching for the door, she lost track of direction. Panic made her miss the hanging vines, and she fled across the slope, searching through the glowing beds of the garden as she heard a whistling and then an outpouring of notes that seemed more like a signal than song, so briefly did it burst forth before fading. *Malia, Malia, Malia,* her fears sang in accompaniment, but her arms and legs felt sluggish, and she seemed the blackest thing in the bright garden of Lampyridae.

"Jarrett," she called, seeing him hurtle past, going the wrong way. But it wasn't he lit by fireflies, not he with the pale hair flying, naked to the waist, with a white bandage.

"Lang!"

He was gone, not having seen her with those wide eyes that looked pitch-black and drugged. She had to go toward the terrible uproar that twisted through the shaft of the winding stair. Her legs were stiff and clumsy. The fireflies confused her steps, and only by stooping near the luminescent fungi could she find the path. Yet her brother had arrowed by her, as if he knew exactly where to go.

Though fearful of what she would see, she staggered forward as the racket diminished. Through radiant lights she glimpsed—once, then again—something white and huge, undulating before her eyes. *Set a snake to catch a snake,* she remembered. Then she was at the gaping jaws of the chimney, where the snapped-off rods were lying on the ground like the aftermath of a violent game of pick-up sticks.

"Lang, Lang—"

There—there he was, kneeling not before a serpent but at the feet of Malia, who stood in a pool of night outside the shining upward rain. She smiled, triumphant, showing the glint of her teeth as she caught sight of Ingledove. But her white dress was dabbled with the indigo of her blood. As the girl watched, she saw Malia twist a stake from her arm and drop it onto the moss, her face aloof, showing no sign of pain. Then her head jerked as she gazed higher up the mountain.

Jarrett's voice was loud in the new quiet, emptied of Malia's clamor. "Whether Phasma Lamia, Lilim child, or Ophis serpent, begone in the name of Sanvi and Sansanvi and Semangelaf, angel messengers of the Maker—"

Malia interrupted him with a trill of laughter as she unlatched a chain around Lang's neck, read the inscription on an amulet, and dropped it. Her fingers showed the fresh marks of burns, as if the necklace had been too hot to touch. "You put this thing around his neck, I gather—so much for your Sanvi, Sansanvi, and Semangelaf! Next time, raise them in person, and then I will be impressed with you, Master Witchmaster." Here she straightened, showing her lovely face. "Come with me, and be my love—there's a line I like! Grant me your names; I'll tell you mine. And if you do, I'll give you something better than your trinkets and toys and books. Wouldn't you like to rest in these arms?" Lifting them toward him, she laughed lightly.

Ingledove stared, afraid that this woman had the power to hoodwink any man—certainly she had lured and taken Lang, who was strong and smart and good. Twice Malia had deceived him, and what she meant to do, who could tell?

"Jarrett, save him!" She heard the voice leave her, as if it were not even hers.

In the streaming light of the fireflies, she saw him race forward and fling a silver-tipped javelin toward the creature. Like colors in the Ulunsuti, the particles of time seemed to slow and break apart, so that she had plenty of opportunity to observe the balanced figure, one arm forward, one leg outstretched behind him, then to turn with agonizing slowness and follow the spear as it swept toward Malia. The young woman seemed to grow taller and more fearsome, her nostrils flaring. Just as the weapon struck her breast and a blue stain soaked her gown, she groaned and altered in appearance, and white coils wrapped around Lang as he and Malia abruptly vanished from sight.

In the Sickroom

"Then you can do nothing, and he will die no matter what—"

"No," Jarrett said; "but he must go to the roots of the mountains, where new things are always being born."

The two of them had scoured the mountainside in the morning, searching for Lang. The Witchmaster had felt certain that Malia would abandon him in the scrub as she had before. Sure enough, he lay flung in a patch of cardinal flower. Dessie spotted them returning with his body, and Ingledove was glad to see her butternut head peering over the precipitous drop. It had taken a long time for Jarrett to scale the cliffs with the weight on his back. Now and then the girl, clambering just above, would warn of loose shale or point to handholds in the stone. She'd managed to rummage up leather pants and a shirt in a small size, outgrown by some long-ago master's boy and right for the bruising job. It was terrifying to her, this thrusting climb depending on fissures and hummocks and the stems of wildflowers.

At the crest of the mountain, Dessie had been waiting with cups of musky-smelling wine. "It'll fortify," she had said, dripping the purple liquid onto Lang's lips. But he hadn't stirred, and even after his wounds were treated, he showed little sign of life.

Ingledove sat silent, watching as the Master ministered to her brother, cleaning the rip in his neck, the paired marks on his shoulder. Under the mild lamplight, Lang was as remote as death, his skin blackened around the first injury and already turning purple at the sites of the new wounds. Only when Jarrett sewed the slash with fine thread did the patient stir and protest. It was a relief to the girl to see him in pain—oh, everything was upside down! The Witchmaster was competent, she thought, better than Danagasta at treating a hurt tenderly. He scanned the bottles in the leather case and picked one or the other with assurance. Why not? He had compounded each of the medicines himself. There was a chamber for just that purpose with floor-to-ceiling racks of vials and a microscope and a set of brass scales.

She was too bone-tired to wonder what he meant by a journey to the roots of the mountains. Whatever he prescribed, she would do if it could save her brother.

"But there's danger in travels," Jarrett mused. "Malia. I'm sure that name's just an anagram for *lamia*."

"What's that?"

"The lamia is a shapeshifter, sometimes a woman, sometimes a snake, sometimes a bit of each. They've been known since classical times. And Malia may try to destroy you, because it's written that such creatures will murder children, and you're in-between, still a girl."

"What about you?"

"Yes, there's a risk for me, too. The Lamia likes to charm men, and she has a certain magnetism. But she's a false monster. I have knowledge and tools against her. The worst thing is that my staff is broken. I'm only half a witchmaster without it, and there's no time to make another, or mend this one—if it can ever be repaired. Why did it come into my head to throw the thing?"

"Maybe because it was the right thing to do," Ingledove said softly. She remembered how his face had gone shocked and still as he saw what had happened—the wood had been riven from top to bottom, exposing the swirling grain of the heart, mysteriously inscribed with minute letters. It was shattered by the contact with Malia, as swiftly as she had crushed Lang. Ingledove touched her brother's cheek. Any flame of anger or resentment that she had ever felt toward him was dead—any reproach she might have given to someone so heedless. A boy of seventeen was no match for the creature she had witnessed through a veil of fireflies, a being lovely but blood-flecked and capable of transformation, her legs fusing and lengthening into the whip of a tail that had curled around her victim with a speed astonishing to see.

As Ingledove bent and kissed him on the forehead, the act seemed a farewell, and she felt grief's undertow drag at her, as if to pull her into darkness. Blinking, she stepped away from the bed. It was possible to drown in such a breaker of feeling; she wanted to give in and cry until she fell to sleep. But she fought the urge as she would have thrust at a serpent's tail winding about her ankles; there was no time for weeping, not when a journey lay ahead.

"Will you go with us?" She whispered, afraid her voice would shiver into tears.

Jarrett had closed the case of vials and begun reading in a big leather-bound notebook. She had peeped in earlier and seen the jottings of past masters, handwritten passages in faded walnut or green or violet ink. "I had forgotten that snakes hate wild parsnip. I wonder." After staring across the room at the unconscious boy, he returned to the page. "This trip will be dangerous. There's a fearsome light in the founts under the hills—by which some have been drawn and lost—a sort of blazing star. The records say that one should glance just at its reflection in the underground river because only venomous snakes can safely stare into the heart of the fire. There's more, but I'll tell you later, when we're nearer the place. And though I'll feed the Ulunsuti immediately before we depart, I'll have to return in seven days. Otherwise I will find out whether or not the Uktena comes back to life as a dragon of fire. I wouldn't like to test the prophecy . . .

"You ask whether I will go. Did you doubt it? Why wouldn't I? It's what I do—tend to Adantis as best I can, according to the laws and rites and sacred formulas handed down from the Old World settlers and the Cherokee."

"But we're not really Adantans, not the way Dessie and Knox are."

He straightened, his eyes still fixed on the page. "Where else do you belong? The houses along Hazel Creek were burned and flooded with water, or dismantled and carried away. Can you live at the bottom of the lake? Do you belong in the house of that man you told me about—the Copper Baron? The woman you call Danagasta was no doubt sent by the previous Master, a man referred to as Loosestrife by the Hidden People. Someday I'll root through his journals and make sure, but probably he saw your mother in the Ulunsuti. She was Adantan, and I imagine that she was homesick before she became ill, and her longings called to the crystal. It's nigh impossible to leave and not be pining forever. But the land along the creek belongs to us now—did you know that?—so her grave is on Adantan soil again. When foreigners barred your way by making the drowned lands a kind of moat, we returned and claimed the district as our own. Or so I've been told by travelers. I've never seen the spot."

So Adantis had lapped around her mother's body, reaching out and restoring the lost child to her own place. That was a blessing, wasn't it? One small glad thing had come of the destruction of the towns. And so a witchmaster must have sent Danagasta to them! If they made it through the mountains and across the reservoir to the train and on to Asheville, she would find out what the old woman knew. Danagasta had told her that her mother wanted to go home, hadn't she? Maybe Marm had wanted the children to be there; she couldn't quite recall. But it hadn't turned out the way Marm would have meant. She never would have intended for Lang to be lying in the Witchmaster's house, inert as granite.

"How will we carry him?"

"I'll fix him enough to travel. It will be tiring for him, pushed on by potions when what he wants is the weaving together that comes with a long rest. His nerves are as exposed as new warp on a loom. I could wake him now, but he needs sleep. A journey won't be good for him, not right away, yet I think we must go—there's no other choice unless we want to see Malia tantalize and devour him. And then her interest would change to us."

Slapping the book shut, he set it aside and took another glance at the patient before leaving the room. Ingledove claimed her brother's hand, but it was heavy and drooped and fell to the bed without making any motion to acknowledge her presence.

She closed the door and ventured to the front chamber. Jarrett had lifted the veil and was gazing into the crystal once again. Rainbows glimmered at the Ulunsuti's heart; then the two figures came into view for an instant, and the girl was fascinated and embarrassed to see that they kissed before dissolving into a flurry of colors.

"It is my fault," he said, "the fault of loneliness, desire, all that—I can't get what I saw out of my head long enough to bring on a different prophecy."

He draped the cloth on the stone, and when he turned away, he gave the girl a long look. She could feel the faint heat of a blush. Though reluctant to ask, she wanted to know what he thought; perhaps he was trying to see the woman's face in hers. Or perhaps there was another Ingledove with fair hair and hazel eyes out there, somewhere. Maybe the vision was all a mistake. She could not tell whether that idea made her glad or sorry.

The couch was now spread with clothes and bunches of herbs and stoppered bottles, which he began to organize. She watched the Witchmaster's steady, methodical packing. His rucksack would be neater than hers, each vial and bandage at hand when required. After a few minutes of silence, she drew away the covering from the Ulunsuti, the feeder vein looking like a scarlet string through the clear stone. The pair was visible in a stream of bright motes, a white dress blurring against a man's shirt so that she could hardly tell where one ended and the other began. The woman's hair was coming unpinned from the braided knot at her neck. Wobbling, the image flew apart and streamed together again. Now the streak of red seemed to drive straight through the woman's body, cutting her in half. But in another instant the clear edges melted, and what had been a man and a woman was only falling snow, which paused, swirled, and re-formed into a single burning star, strung on a bloody thread.

Slowly she let the flowery cloth descend over the rock. Jarrett had paused in his packing and was watching, though when she turned toward him, he resumed work.

Impulsively she went to him. There was no room on the couch, so she knelt on the floor, laying a hand on his wrist.

"I'm sorry," she told him; "I'm really sorry."

He looked at her and nodded, a flush of red on his cheeks. After a minute he rose and crossed to the fireplace to take down the presentation sword.

TO THE ROOTS OF THE MOUNTAINS

"Not far," the Witchmaster had said.

Ingledove slipped the pack from her shoulders and watched him peel a forked stick.

It had been far, by her measuring—terribly far; they had set out before dawn, while Lampyridae's garden smoldered in the moss. Jarrett had gone first, winding down the stairs to the jumping-off place in the laurel where they would meet up with the path. He had fastened a mesh bag of the enchanted fireflies to his pack, and by that glimmering light they plunged into the chasm. A cloud of insects had hovered above the chimney's mouth and, as if summoned by their imprisoned fellows, began flooding into the gap, twisting into the depths of the fissure and rising again until the shaft was luminous and moon-bright. This had seemed like a fair start, and Lang's feet were sure along the steps, although his face was pale and his eyes glittering.

Once, when he had stopped and his sister had paused on the step just above his, he laughed and said, "What a peculiar dream."

In the laurel hell below the shaft, just before he sprang onto the trail, Jarrett had untied the mesh and set the insects free. In seconds they were gone, all but the last few that clung to the sack or crawled on the Witchmaster's arms and braided hair, as if they wanted to stay with him and go farther into the wilderness.

"They'll die if they pass beyond the bounds of my land— this is where Lampyridae's magic ends," he had told the girl, who didn't see why they shouldn't travel over the mountains in a fog of brightness. He had flicked them away and waited until the last one flew into the thicket. Only then had he leaped to the trail below the laurel, the chief's sword flashing as he arced to the ground.

"Funny to get light from decay," Lang had said.

"What does he mean?" his sister had asked. She had taken to asking Jarrett about her brother, because the injured boy now spoke seldom and unexpectedly and rarely answered a question unless it was repeated three or four times.

"Just the chemical mating of luminescence. A luciferin plus oxygen is excitable, so it decays and emits light."

"That name's like Lucifer?"

"Yes, it's *luciferin*. I suppose he was shining once, when he was a heavenly angel. Or maybe he still is—maybe he shines in corruption. We Adantans believe in Lucifer as well as in the Maker. The Old World borderers around the Baltic Sea learned that he populated the world with fell beings like Malia. Even before the emigrants mingled with the native people, the Cherokee knew that the mountains were sacred but places of risk, their secret coves alive with spirits and wizards. Subtle beings like the raven mockers, who steal life from the sick and injured, can wear a harmless shape. When the settlers and the Cherokee became the Hidden People and Adantis was created, none of these beliefs passed away, because the ridges and valleys kept their magnetic pull on otherworldly creatures, whether good or ill. Maybe that sounds strange to you, growing up as one of the outlandish."

"No, that sounds like Danagasta," she had replied. "Anyway, there are bad things in Asheville and everywhere."

"It's my feeling that the outlanders know the aspect of evil that arises from their nature and ways, as we Adantans know the sort that emerges from ours."

They trudged with candle lanterns until dawn came and Lang grew sluggish. Though dosed throughout the morning, he became more and more lethargic in his movements, until they were forced to let him sleep during the noon hour. When he woke, he would eat nothing, though he willingly drank the Witchmaster's medicines.

"I don't like it. It's a bad sign that he doesn't want food—human food, anyway. He'll be livelier as the sun starts to drop, I'd guess. That's leading toward the hours that are Malia's. At least we've seen no sign of her." Jarrett had spoken in a low voice, eyes on his patient, who was standing with head cocked, as if straining to hear something very far away.

"It's best that you know," he had added.

"What else is there?"

"I've spotted ravens twice, but they've kept well away. Perhaps they're only birds. Or maybe they're just spies."

The girl had glanced toward her brother. "Could they know that he belongs to *her*?"

"That, too, was my thought."

They had tried to outwit the Lamia, hiking in streams wherever the bed was level. Lang had struggled to walk on the slippery rocks, leaning on Jarrett, but after three o'clock he moved more easily, and each hour that passed gave him renewed strength. Not long before dusk they reached their goal, the foot of a mountain that to Ingledove appeared no different from any other. She collapsed on a low tablet of stone in a nearby creek, stripping off her high boots and socks and rolling up the loose britches she had found during another foray into the storage chests. The pants had been better for walking through briars than Danagasta's dresses. With the thin linen tucked inside her boots, they made her feel immune to ticks and biting insects. The Witchmaster didn't mind, though he said she'd have to pass as a boy if they met any Adantans. She gave the cuffs one last twist and plunged her reddened feet into the icy water.

"Come sit." She called to Lang several times before he responded. "It feels wonderful."

He halted, barefoot, boots in one hand; he passed the other over his eyes, as if to clear his vision. "Something doesn't want me to—doesn't like the stream."

Alarmed, she scanned the mountainsides but saw nothing except a raven, hanging in the air. "All the more reason to come enjoy it," she told him, wading across and grasping his hand.

Jarrett, overhearing, came toward them, paring the bark

from a stick. "I guess she's awake now, if she's influencing him. But I don't think that there's anything here to worry about; I don't feel anything amiss, and I'm pretty good at knowing— usually a lot better than I was when Malia snaked through the stairs. Lampyridae's garden was so busy telling me something was the matter that I didn't notice a change."

He joined them in the water, soaking his feet, which the girl noticed were thin and pale. "You need better boots," he told her. "Mine are handmade by Corley Terrell, the most fa- mous bootsmith in Adantis. But it's all right. Once we find the tunnels of the Yunwi Tsunsdi, you can tie yours to a pack and go barefoot, because the floors will be smooth and cool. At least if these tunnels are like the others I've seen."

"Yunwi," she repeated.

"The Little People. They were great tunnelsmiths in earlier times, though I don't think they're so active anymore. Maybe they have all the ways of going that they need."

"Marm used to talk about them! I never thought they were real, just some of her stories. I know what you mean—the Cherokee fairies. Well, they're not so very tiny, the way people often imagine fairies, but they're small." For a moment Ingle- dove longed for her mother, remembering how they would sit on the porch bench while she told fantastic tales. To think that they might've been true! Why hadn't Marm gone home to Adantis after they were abandoned? Was she too proud to ad- mit what had happened? It was sad to think that her daughter would never know.

"Lang . . ."

He hadn't heard and still seemed to be rapt, his legs ankle-deep in the flow. The water was freezing, and she thought he must be numb by now. She dipped her feet in and out of the rushing current, unable to bear the constant brunt of cold.

"That's right," Jarrett said, inspecting the branch in his hands. "The Little People are known even outside Adantis. Some of their tunnels have been destroyed by builders with bulldozers, and their bones have sometimes been found. Loosestrife once recovered a pair of skulls and some bones from the outlander school in Cullowhee. They were set out on a desk like something meant for show, but he wrapped the remains in new linen and carried them home and left them in the mouth of a tunnel. He always said that the Little People live to a great age but can be killed. I don't know why anyone would want to do such a thing."

Meticulously he scraped the last streaks of brown from the wand.

"That's a dowsing rod, isn't it—hazel?"

"Yes—and no, there's no hazel or willow at hand. I clipped a twig off a silverbell tree. I don't remember ever seeing a silverbell in this area before, but they like to bloom where it's damp. The Little People might've planted it, so I asked if—"

"What's the wand for? Why do we need one here?"

"For seeking underground—not much different from a fellow hunting for where to put a well near his cabin." He twirled the peeled stick in his hands. "I always prefer a fresh-cut limb. The moist sap calls to buried springs." He slipped the knife in his pocket. "Thought I'd have to skin it with the sword until I found my blade."

"I know about dowsing. But why now? You didn't answer my question." Although she'd longed to reach a destination,

Ingledove felt more anxious than she had earlier, now that they had come to a stop.

"The tunnels we want to find dive through the earth to a watery region, and according to Loosestrife's notes, this is the way to find them."

"You've never been here . . ."

"Nope. Not exactly here. Not even once. I've been, oh, a few hundred yards away, and I've wanted to visit the tunnels. The ones I've seen before were real marvels, dipping through the clay and stone, perfectly shaped. But I've never tried to find them. You don't bother the spirit races without need."

He stood and wandered off barefoot, wading through a drift of flowering spurge and fireweed. She watched his progress for a while, until her attention was drawn to her brother, who was lying on a boulder, his feet still immersed in the water.

"Lang, you won't be able to walk . . ."

She waded over to him and dragged his feet from the stream. They were so wrinkled and white that she felt worried, shoving them onto the stone. As she had expected, he didn't move but stayed with his legs propped, knees up.

When the Witchmaster passed by she called to him, gesturing to the cold feet.

"Hyperemia," he said, looking her way for an instant. "He'll be all right. They'll be turning red soon."

He meandered on, moving closer to the wall of the mountain. Ingledove wanted to follow and watch as he dowsed. She had seen the stick tremble; there must be an aquifer here, to make it so prone to move. When she spoke, she realized that her brother was already asleep—well, that was fine, so long as he didn't dream about Malia. Probably he was too tired for dreams. The rocks were still warm with the sun, and his feet would return to normal. She didn't think he would roll into the creek and drown; she had never seen someone so heavy and unstirring in sleep. Reluctantly she put on her socks and shoes, finding that they didn't feel so bad now that her feet were no longer swollen from walking. Telling Lang that he should wait because she would be only a few minutes—and feeling silly for talking to someone so unresponsive—she zigzagged over the rough ground, beggar-lice catching on her pants and bootlaces.

"Have you found something?" She reached Jarrett's side; he held the wand loosely, the wide V of the prongs lying on his palms. The point was moving slowly and steadily downward. "That's not how water witching was done on Hazel Creek. You're holding the branch wrong."

"No, this is real 'wishing' or 'witching.' Dowsers who grip the prongs can force the stick to bend—though I imagine that mostly they come to a spot that looks promising, like a site where they've found water before, and the whole movement of the wand is unconscious. It's pointing at the cliff." He shifted his feet and the divining rod moved to one side, steady in its convictions.

"Did Lang fall asleep?" He cast a swift glance at the girl.

She nodded. "He looked dead to the world."

"Well, he's not. But I want to get him inside the mountain before dusk arrives, and he becomes more wakeful. That's when Malia may try to find and lure him away with her singing. She was hurt last night, but she won't stay holed up in her lair. You know how Lang felt stopped by the creek? Evidently she doesn't like running water, but the need to cross streams won't slow her up for long." He surveyed the rock closely. "Rub your hand over the base and see if you feel anything out of the ordinary."

Sitting on her heels, Ingledove ran her fingers across the uneven stone. Little silvery flecks and embedded violet gems caught her eye, but she felt no selvage between wall and door, nothing that resembled an entrance.

"There's an inscription! I didn't see it at first . . ."

As if reading her mind, he added, "Or maybe it wasn't there before."

He stabbed the wish stick into the earth and knelt beside her. "The upper one's Cherokee, but it's almost obliterated by lichens. All I can make out is *Sge*."

"This one's English!" she exclaimed, feeling as glad as if they'd found a treasure in the forest. The two bent, picking out the words:

Ku!

If you have need,
Then pay a heed
And gain a meed.

If you mean wrong,
Then ponder long
Where you belong.

If you have doubt
And laws would flout—
Then turn about.

But if you must,
O mortal dust,
Receive our trust,

Which if you break,
A starry lake
Of blood will slake

The thirst awake
In spot and strake,
All for our sake.

"Not very hospitable, are they?" She interrupted the pieced-together words. "It seems that everything involves blood these days."

The Master let out a crooked smile as he picked a ruffle of lichen from the next letters. "Maybe they're just being realistic."

"What about *meed* and *strake*? I don't even know what those are."

"They're a bit old-fashioned. *Meed* is a reward. I'm not so sure about *strake*—I think it means a streak of color."

You wish to dare
The wilding air
Of the most fair?

Be fleet to run
Below the sun
Till life is won

Or lost—three hands
On stone in lands
Of spirit bands

Will let you in
And, lose or win,
Back out again.

"You saw us in the Ulunsuti," she said, forgetting to feel a shyness about the prophetic images. "Doesn't that mean we'll survive whatever's here?"

"Not necessarily. It shows what may be—remember?—if all goes well." The Witchmaster set his palms against the stone. "Add a hand to mine. Just right there so our fingertips touch, one upright, two above. The Little People like things to be orderly. Well, not *orderly* exactly, but nicely, meaningfully arranged. There's an artistic streak in them."

"A *strake*." She whispered the words as she slid her fingers across the pitted surface.

It was no use. However they arranged their hands, no door opened.

"We need to fetch Lang," Jarrett said. "I was hoping that it was just any three hands. Then it wouldn't matter if somebody didn't return—"

"What? It would matter—"

"Yes, I know. I just mean that if, say, I died, you and your brother could open the door."

Ingledove leaned her forehead against the cold rock. She knew what he had meant, and she was frightened. *If Lang died* was surely his first thought. Gazing at the sky, she saw the moon, caught in its familiar cycles of wax and wane. Who knew about anything? Maybe on that pristine globe, unmarred by the footprints of men, there were elvish tribes going about their mysterious businesses, or fearsome dragons of the sun, or luminous children frolicking in the faraway craters. World and universe seemed bigger and more filled with possibilities than she had ever dreamed, but she didn't like the widening gulf of the unknown.

"Maybe it just means hands, anyway," he went on. "The Little People can be very literal. You could always chop off one of mine with the sword and press it to the wall."

"That's the most disgusting thing I've ever thought about," she said, standing to tighten the purple sash to her shirt. "Let's go wake Lang."

Then suddenly she feared that he had tumbled into the water and drowned, so they dashed across the valley floor. And there he was, asleep with his feet still planted on the boulder and the waves splashing over pebbles. Jarrett waded the stream and recovered the boots and packs, handing a share to Ingledove. Even though the sleeping boy woke and followed them without a word, she found that her uneasiness was not yet allayed, because the sun was starting to slide on its arc behind the mountains, and the dusk was almost upon them. She remembered that her brother would be more alert when twilight came because that was the hour when Malia would stir and come hunting for prey.

Just as they gained the cliff, she heard a faraway burst of notes. She felt as if they showered ice into her very bones. Putting an arm around Lang's waist, she exchanged a glance with Jarrett, who was listening, his mouth slightly ajar as if he needed a little more air than usual.

"Three hands on the stone," he said in a low voice.

The silver in the rock flickered like stars as they fitted their right hands together—"nothing possibly sinister, no lefts," the Master had said—and the surface began to pulse and fly into atoms. But not particles, no, these were winged creatures that glittered and rose toward a sky that was only now dusk enough for Venus to be seen.

"Fireflies . . ."

It was her brother who had spoken and was beaming in the midst of the flares of silver and purple light, his curled fingers cradling a tiny silver being. More of them had caught on his open shirt and were crawling across the blue-black star below his collarbone. To Ingledove, it seemed that the mark was subtly smaller than before.

"Come on, Lang." She had tears in her eyes as she pushed him gently through the moving veil and turned to look outside. All she could see was a dazzle of silver and purple until she blotted her eyes and glimpsed the air turning blue beyond the doorway and the wand still driven in the ground. Then a waterfall of wings dashed over the archway and hid the mountains and sky from view. It shimmered for a few moments and settled into darkness except for a few gleams of silver that went on winking, lending a faint illumination to the tunnel.

"Lang, Lang," the Witchmaster said. "*Fireflies.* That was a true voice of wonder. I haven't heard such a thing from my own throat for years."

THE FIRST AND SECOND DAYS

In the tunnels there was neither day nor night, only the constant glitter in the stone. Lang discovered that if he brushed against the wall or touched the low roof, a spark would fly out, and a glinting insect would come to his hand and climb his sleeve to settle on the black star. In the first hour he became encrusted with the little creatures, so that the wounds on his neck and shoulder and the blaze below the collarbone were entirely sheathed in silver. The star sparkled through the loose weave of his shirt. Even Ingledove's sore feet drew the fireflies, who winged her heels with their metal.

"Leave them be," the Witchmaster advised. "They won't harm. And who knows? The Yunwi Tsunsdi who made the tunnels are famous healers."

Those were not the only sources of light, for narrow rivulets coursed along the sides of the passageways, sometimes crossing and plunging into a narrow branch; in their rapid, shallow waters the dazzle of the roof and walls was reflected like the constellations in a stream. An almost imperceptible slant to the floor sent them flowing along the corridors.

Jarrett had brought one of Lampyridae's inventions, a shining reel that unspooled its contents when commanded, "Thread of *nunda sunna yehi*, stay and go!" Fastening itself to the door, the luminous spool vanished into a pocket, where it quietly went on unrolling a substance like radiant embroidery floss, marking a path and lending light to their feet.

Ingledove was glad to see this frail string, because she had secretly wondered whether they could find the way to the door again, should the Master die. Now and then he had to stop to consult a piece of folded parchment containing a map of the tunnels. Jarrett treated the paper with great care, saying that it had once belonged to Inadunai, who as a boy had had the friendship and affection of the Little People. Peeping over his arm, she saw what looked like a tree of dense tangled boughs, topped by a crown of leaves.

They walked for several hours the first evening, though they were already tired. Only Lang seemed lively, his interest moving whimsically from the fireflies to the thread to the streamlets beside the path, from which he dredged fine pinpricks of luminescence that swam on his palm and, when poured into a puddle, swarmed like bees.

"He feels better. Maybe he *is* better," Ingledove whispered to Jarrett as they paused to rest, watching Lang paddling his fingers in a pool on the tunnel floor. "But he doesn't act like himself—or he's more like he was when we were little and lived on Hazel Creek. Even that's not what he is—he seems so different."

"He's stronger than he was a day ago. That doesn't mean he's anywhere near well. Venom from the Lamia is still being shunted through his body." The Witchmaster touched the thread with his finger, making certain that it still held firm. "If he gets over this, he'll be more like himself. But he'll never be exactly the same—who could be?"

When the girl felt that she could go no farther, her legs having grown stiff and chilled, they lay on the floor between two channels of water and slept, cauled in some thin warm bags brought from the house in the mountain. Just before the tide of sleep pulled her under, she heard her brother singing low and tuneless under his breath:

> I wandered in the Silverwood—
> A stain was in my blood
>
> Because I'd kissed a girl like snow,
> And ever since, a glow
>
> Of icy fire has scorched my heart,
> Consumed by her black art.

So utterly worn in body and mind that she could barely move and hardly knew whether she was waking or sleeping, Ingledove turned her head to look at Lang. He was smiling as hundreds of wings darted toward him, the insects seeking him out with such speed that they left gilt trails on the air. They clustered lovingly on his face and set shining mail over every inch of his body. He was an image of death: an armored knight on a tomb; a mummy dressed in silver leaf. The girl blinked, searching for a sign of familiar life. But they sealed his lips and weighted his lids until he obeyed and closed his eyes.

As she began to call for Jarrett, a few of the tiny creatures hovering above her face were swept up by the sharp intake of breath, so that they flew down her throat. After, when she breathed, the air turned silver, and she dreamed that she was the boy Ild, tumbling from a high promontory into a valley of wordless song.

Then she knew this was sleep, and she let go, falling deeper and deeper into a gorge of hush and dark, where just as her feet found the topmost bough of a blossoming sourwood tree, she saw a bright laughing face and another and another.

She felt joyful and opened her mouth to name them *children of light*, because she could no longer recall the name *Yunwi Tsunsdi*, but when she did, a ribbon of silver fireflies poured from her throat and danced around the sourwood tree like streamers of precious metal around a maypole, and she remembered nothing at all.

When she woke, the tunnels were just the same as before. The fine luminous string stretched behind them until it was overcome by blackness. But Lang was better, the injuries on his neck now pale scars, only the first terrible wound remaining as a diminished blaze, blue as indigo. He was not yet himself, seeming as distracted as the day before, squatting by a rivulet, damming it with his foot until gleaming specks collected and shone like coins in a sunny fountain, then letting it swirl into the dark.

"What happened?" Ingledove left her brother's side and knelt by the Witchmaster; he handed her a torn piece of bread and offered some to Lang, who only shook his head.

"What happened was that I had a talk with the Yunwi Tsunsdi in the night—if one can call such oracular snips of news a *talk*. They pop in and out, uttering the gnomic nonsense that might help, if I knew what it meant. 'The third day.' That's somewhat clear. I guess it'll be our third day in the tunnels when we reach our goal. 'Snake can look at star.' That's cryptic. I don't know whether they mean that starry wound on your brother, or maybe the Ulunsuti, or something else. The snake might be the Lamia or the Uktena, though a crowned water serpent with a jewel in its brow is more like a dragon. 'The song is coming.' That must be a warning about Malia. Whether or not their words come clear, the Little People have helped us, because I showed them your brother, and they touched his wounds.

"But I've made a mistake," he continued. "And I feel bad about it. That's three now. I didn't realize that the Lamia was thrusting up through the winding stair, and I broke my staff. And this is bad, too, because she'll arrive more quickly than she would have. It's sheer carelessness—I left the wish stick by the door, and she'll find it."

Ingledove stuffed the last of the crust in her mouth. The bread tasted sweet and briefly reminded her of Dessie. She reflected on the news. "We can't go back. I don't see that it's so terrible," she said at last. "She would get here no matter what, wouldn't she?"

"But if she came later, Lang might be healed, and any encounter with her would be less serious."

"It's not that much worse," the girl decided. "Either way Malia might destroy us all." That was no consolation, yet somehow she felt more hopeful this morning. And for some reason she didn't want to talk about the sight of her brother plated in silver or how the shining faces of the Yunwi Tsunsdi had peered into her dreams.

The day wore on much as the evening before, with Jarrett leading the way, stopping occasionally to check the map by the glow from Lampyridae's line, which sometime in the night had begun to emit a faint humming. Ingledove became accustomed to the shimmer in the walls and ceiling, and now seldom thought about the strangeness of the place. She was still numb and exhausted from the previous day and put one foot ahead of the other like someone walking in sleep. Only Lang showed curiosity during this part of the journey. The Witchmaster kept looking over his shoulder, reminding him to keep up. He might be stock-still, entranced by an insect crawling on the ceiling, or else splashing barefoot through a glaze of water spreading across the floor.

So it went for hours, until at last they heard the tumbling noise of falls.

"We'll stop as soon as we reach here." The bright thread slashed across the parchment. Jarrett traced a finger around the canopy of the tunnel-tree. "This area is called the Cauldron of Flowers. There's a huge staircase—maybe several—in a cavern. Or so it's written by the Masters, and so the Tellers say."

"I'm starved." Ingledove let her pack down with a thump.

The two of them sat on the floor, drinking from a canteen of water and eating the crisp, saffron-dyed bread called *Loosestrife's flowers*. Eventually Lang drifted over and accepted one of the paper-thin blossoms, because, he said, they looked like stars. But his sister noticed that he didn't eat it. After a while he put the yellow bread on the water and let the current carry it away. Like a child, he followed the meanderings of his gift, staying close behind until lost in sequined dark.

"Come back . . ."

The Witchmaster yanked a slender jointed tube and a bag from his pack before he leaped to his feet and dashed after him, vanishing almost instantly. Seeing nothing, Ingledove swung around and looked along the vibrating thread. That was the way out, and the steady beacon of light was comforting. She could hear nothing but the swirl of the dividing stream and the faraway roar coming from the Cauldron of Flowers. She was perched high on Inadunai's headfirst tree— surely that meant she was deep in the roots of the mountains? Rarely had she sensed that they were moving sharply downward, the slow slippage was so gradual and the temperature remained so constant, cool as a cave.

She thought very hard about the map and the tree of tunnels thrusting into the earth, but it didn't distract her from listening. Her brother might have plummeted into a sinkhole, chasing some will-o'-the-wisp, and have been lost forever. And Jarrett was without Lampyridae's spool . . . Somewhere water began drip, drip, dripping from the ceiling. She closed her eyes, feared to open them again—and just as suddenly went wide-eyed, hearing a rustling noise and a rattle. The reel had spilled from the pack and with a flash of silver began to roll and dance away. Panicked, she darted after the thread and caught the little object in her hand. But when she opened her fingers, the spool began to joggle across her palm until it bounced to the floor and went pinwheeling off.

So it's all right, then, I guess. The thing knows where it's going, even if I don't. Just sit and wait.

She thought of coaxing a firefly to her finger but was afraid to move. Marm had always told her to be careful and then she would fear nothing. She remembered lying with her head in her mother's lap, counting the stars, listening to stories of ghosts and fairies and beautiful immortals who watched over a world too busy to pay heed. Until recently, she might have thought those tales wild and fey, but now she knew they were not outlandish but Adantan. Unshed tears burned in her eyes as she realized that since crossing the drowned lands, she had come to understand a different Marm from the one she had loved, who had given the constellations names that nobody else seemed to know—the Glowworm, the Magic Garden, the Sorcerer Raven, the Hair of the Little People. Alone and afraid, she remembered the cluster of seven stars that her mother had called the Gifts. Everyone has gifts, Jarrett had told her. "Let one be bravery," she whispered; "let fear bring courage." After a while she leaned forward and seized the sword, settling it crosswise on her knees. That felt better— knowing that she wasn't helpless seemed a first step. And when she heard a dragging sound, she stood with weapon raised, the glory from the walls burning on its blade.

"It's me . . ."

The voice sounded ghostly, echoing in the tunnel, but it belonged to the Witchmaster. Ingledove lowered the sword. Her shirt felt cold and clung against her back.

In another minute she sped forward, because she could see him half carrying a burden with Lampyridae's spool twirling alongside, reeling in thread.

"Lang!"

She gathered his cold bare feet in her arms and helped lay him on the floor.

"Malia," she whispered, squatting beside her brother, who looked pale and panicky. A bluish stain was spreading on his shirt.

"He'll be fine. He's even almost all right now. She barely nicked him, though the old hurt was tender and bled. And I've made her angry." Jarrett knelt with one hand on the ground, catching his breath, and added, "I drove her off with a miniature blowgun, a child's toy." He dropped the tube and sack of darts. "And silver points feathered with dried parsnip blossoms. It won't keep a lamia at bay forever, but it's irritating to her, especially shot near the eyes. Glad I was reminded that snakes hate wild parsnip."

He worked quickly, cleaning the chest of blood and smearing ointment on the wound. A fresh bandage bound over one shoulder nearly covered the blue star.

"I don't know why she bit in the same spot as before," he muttered. "Maybe she meant to kill this time. But she didn't get much of a chance."

"We never heard her."

"Oh, she can quietly lurk in a hole until we pass by. I've been watching the tunnels carefully so that she couldn't surprise us. It's too bad, when he's so weak from lack of food."

Ingledove held her brother's hand as Jarrett pulled a bundle of limp wild parsnip from the bottom of his pack and started weaving a necklace. He fastened the wreath around the victim's neck and pinned a thumb-sized twist of fabric above his heart.

"What's that?"

"A traditional amulet containing a bit of shed Uktena skin, young raven's down, and a scrap of paper containing a name of the Maker: *the Holy One of the Mountains.*"

"Does it do anything?"

"Names are powerful. If your brother hadn't given his own so easily, he might not be in this fix."

"What now?"

He didn't answer but helped Lang to sit and drink from a bottle of evil-smelling medicine. A few of the fireflies had floated from the ceiling and now settled near the injury. After watching them trundle about the bandage, the Witchmaster untied the linen bindings and let the insects settle on the malignant star. One by one, others flew to the sick boy until the rays were not blue but entirely silver. Then they began alighting on the parsnip wreath, crawling on the stems until it was a massive breastplate of living metal. Last, a few of the rare purple insects, which they had not seen since entering the tunnels, wavered along the glowing road of Lampyridae's filament and aimed for the very heart of the star.

Lang cupped one in his hands and held it near the spool. He stared at the tiny being, scintillating in the light.

"I love them."

Ingledove could not have been more surprised to hear such a claim from her brother's mouth. Had she ever heard him say such a word as *love* about anyone or anything? He had been passionate but not inclined to tenderness. Perhaps it was a measure of how sick he had become.

"Who knows where they come from and go? But their faces look . . ." He stopped, gazing into his hands. "I don't know how they look."

It was the most he had spoken in a long time. Inspecting the glinting head, the girl felt surprised to see that he was right—how human it appeared, the features elflike, the lidded eyes particularly unlike those of an insect.

"Aren't they fireflies?"

Jarrett watched as one haloed Lang's head and came to rest on his hair. "Maybe they're an aspect of the Yunwi Tsunsdi. Maybe they flew from the throne of the Giver. Maybe they come from elsewhere. It's not written in the Masters' histories.

"As for *what now*," he continued, "I think we'll have to gain the Cauldron tonight and sleep on its brink, at the top of the staircase. That will be safer, closer to powers that can protect us. Tomorrow we may glimpse an Uktena, the Yunwi Tsunsdi, or the Yunwi Amayinehi, and that will be more marvels than most Adantans see in a lifetime in the mountains. Don't ask me any more—no matter how tired you are or how weak your brother is, we must go. And you'll see soon enough." Speaking with intensity, he added a warning: "Just remember, never, never look into the crown of the Uktena. Its fire is too strong for mortals. In a letter, James Mooney wrote, 'There the talismanic Ulunsuti sets his dragonish serpent's face ablaze.' " Jarrett heaved a pack onto his shoulders and reached for the sword.

Still seated, Ingledove gazed at his face, deeply shadowed and stern in the dimness of the tunnel. For the first time she thought how impressive he appeared, every line of his body speaking of resolution. He was girded for a fight. And remembering that he had used the sword before, she hoped that a struggle might not be so one-sided as it had seemed when she glimpsed the Lamia at Lampyridae's garden, bloody but defiant. She rose to her feet, sure of her course. She would not fail him or her brother. She would do what she could.

Lang had heard nothing of the Witchmaster's words. As he smiled at the silver firefly, the look of naked delight on his face made him seem alien to her again, as if he were nobody she knew. Where was the schoolboy of seventeen, the smart determined one who teased and was sometimes cruel and angry and impetuous, who already felt himself to be a man, with a man's rights and obligations? She wanted him—that one, even with his faults.

Yet this one was still her big brother. *And a child of Adantis,* she thought. *Like me and Marm.*

The insect had climbed onto his sleeve and was making an ascent to the lustrous star on his chest. Head bent to watch, the motionless boy seemed fascinated by the delicacy of the creature's motions and the splendor of its tiny face, still uplifted.

"Come on, Lang." His sister laced her fingers with his and tugged, leading him into the dark glitter.

THE CAULDRON OF FLOWERS

The humming of Lampyridae's line disturbed Ingledove's sleep, and she woke, remembering that they lay directly over the cavern that was their destination. Jarrett had insisted on the shelf of rock, saying that they would be safer sleeping in the mist rising from the pool below. She lay with her eyes shut, listening to the melodious lapping of water. Low waterfalls spilled into the bowl, and all around was a melody made by trickling rivulets. Now she could hear tiny outcries, like needles pricking at the silken fabric of sound.

That didn't seem right; nor did the noise in the line, which gave out a loud plucked note, a perfect middle C.

As if weighted by coins, her lids felt heavy, heavy. But what she saw by the light from the thread and the Cauldron of Flowers made her eyes widen.

Reptilian with no trace left of woman except for a pair of red lips, Malia had crept into their midst and draped herself over Lang's throat. His inert body stared glassy-eyed and sightless; the snake's jaws had fastened onto the blue star of wound, abandoned by the fireflies—who were moiling so thickly about the Witchmaster that Ingledove couldn't detect any of him, though she could see the serpent's face a yard from her own only too clearly. The textured head looked oddly fabricated, as if stitched with white yarn in a closely worked needlepoint pattern of diamonds. The narrow tongue licked the large blue drops that had formed like a dew on her brother's skin. Feeling helpless, trapped in her sleeping bag without a weapon, she stared at the scaly body, still showing gouges from the barrier at the top of the gyring stair and an explosion of blue under the skin where the staff had rammed through her flesh. The Lamia knew the girl could do nothing, for it smiled at her. A little eye watched her without blinking. She remembered that snakes were said to hypnotize their prey. A larval heaviness seemed to drift through her, as if she were losing her ability to stir, cauled in a cocoon.

The swarming of the insects increased, and suddenly she glimpsed a blade slashing through confining cloth; Jarrett sprang to his feet, instantly armored in fireflies, who continued to emit the microscopic cries that had helped awaken her. The Lamia's head rose lazily over its victim, lips dark with blood.

The Master leaped forward, the sword upraised as he called out,

> *Little worm,*
> *Little infant slug,*
> *Little soft caterpillar—*

Snowflake in the sun—
False color of peace!
Before the light sinks
You will be wholly blue.

Little worm,
Demon-born—
Thing without soul—
Foe of the Maker—
A rain of blue clay,
A rain of black clay
Will pelt your skin.

His voice became stronger, echoing in the cavern. The fluid silver encasing his body shifted restlessly, a few of the insects flying about his head in excited orbits. With another leap, he struck, shouting out the final words:

The blue veil,
The black stone
Will cover your head
In the Darkening Land!

The blade slid easily into the flesh, which grew cloudy and transparent. Seeing that the Lamia was about to disappear, Ingledove threw herself out of the bag, clutching after the tail that switched angrily on the floor. The spirit being let out a shriek as hands sank into her melting substance. Then the sword slashed through the swirling white, dispersing its particles until there was nothing left.

"Is she dead?" The echo of the cry tingled in the girl's ears. Small blue dots flecked her palms.

"No, not that one."

Jarrett had cast away the sword and was crouching beside Lang. "One more time and she'll have him, I'm afraid."

The insects were beginning to drop from the Witchmaster onto the injured boy, tickling his brow with their tiny steps. As they covered his hair with a shining helmet, Lang's eyes moved for the first time, coming to rest on his sister.

If a glance can break your heart, that is it, she thought, taking his hand. It was the look of someone who has suffered a long time with patience: a mute, enduring expression. He had accepted his condition, the horror and the pain of it, and was ready for whatever would come—even his own death.

"This will be a chancy thing," the Master said, sitting back on his heels to examine the injury. "But we'll cheat her in the end, I hope."

Cheat her of Lang? she wondered.

"I think you may have harmed her, plunging your fingers into that smoke of dissolving flesh. Spirit beings are more fragile when between forms. An innocent hand, groping in her serpentine vitals—that may have lamed the Lamia, at least for now." He nodded at her. "Will you fetch some things out of my pack? A bottle marked *Aristolochia serpentaria*, poultice of snakeroot, mixed with zinc and herbs potent against infection. A vial labeled *oil of calendula*. And some clean linen."

Catching sight of her speckled palms, he seized and examined them closely and tried to wipe a blot away.

"Wash them. It seems harmless, but caution's best. Blue is an unpropitious color for Adantans. Still, maybe that's a good

sign for us, since she is the source of it. She gave him the indigo star, and she has drunk from its trouble and filth."

Was he uneasy? She couldn't tell but scrubbed in a puddle,
even dipping up the shining gilt and rubbing the abrasive stuff
against her skin. But she stayed as stained as before. By then
the Witchmaster had sluiced Lang's chest with water and studied the fresh change to the wound; he was ready for the bottle
of snakeroot.

It cost them an hour to tend the bite, eat, and pack. Ingledove thought that morning must have come, for light reflected off the pool beneath them sent enormous wavering
panels of shine and shadow across the cavern walls, and while
she readied herself to go, the atmosphere grew noticeably sun-
nier, though she could find no rift in the ceiling. With fresh illumination, it became apparent that the cave was quarried
from a white stone, though it glimmered at times like sapphire
or amethyst, even glowing as rosily as the mountain rubies
that were called *pigeon's blood*. Streaks of green shot through
the air, and the chamber altered in intensity as swiftly as a fading and brightening rainbow. While her brother slept, she lay
at the brink of the eastern staircase and watched the colors
mutate as she finished Loosestrife's flowers and drank water
scooped from the streams, a sediment of gilt at the bottom of
the cup. The Cauldron was deeper and wider than she had
imagined, rounded but impressively canyonlike in its dimen-
sions. Vertigo made her close her eyes against the far-off floor,
though the very sight of clear waves dancing with golden
motes made her feel refreshed, so that she imagined it to be an
easy thing to descend the long stairs and go skipping into the
pool at the base, although the water might not be as shallow

as the streams that frisked the length of the staircases and trickled down the walls.

The bread tasted sweeter than ever this morning, and Dessie drifted into her mind, followed by Danagasta, a far-away figure busy in the Copper Baron's kitchen on baking day. If she had stayed safely at home—except that someone else's house could never be more than a borrowed nest—none of this would have happened. Or would events somehow have come to such a pass anyway? Had they begun before the brother and sister crossed the doorstep? She remembered Danagasta's song mocking the ghost snake in Lang's dream. Jarrett had said such songs were sacred formulas, handed down from the Cherokee and woven with ideas from the Old World. She supposed that Marm's children were truly Adantans, made from the two peoples, the two cultures. If she stayed in the mountains, she would learn what that meant. Perhaps they had relatives there, tucked behind a bank of doghobble or burrowed under a boulder shingled in lichens.

On the far edge of the cave, another staircase zigzagged from ceiling to the floor, pausing for balconies and landings. Danagasta hated cleaning the Copper Baron's grand stair with the railings around the top, but it was nothing compared to the two entrances into the Cauldron.

"I'd like to see her polish that one," she murmured. Biting into the very last of Loosestrife's flowers, her eyes on the walls opposite, she saw a door open at the apex of the stairs. For a moment she half expected to see Danagasta come bustling out with a rag and a jar of homemade beeswax polish. Instead, a troupe of small figures carrying baskets of white blossoms gathered on the landing. As one began to sing in a piercing, childlike voice, fireflies flew from the mouths of tunnels. They soon vanished in the distance, only an occasional silver blink showing that they had been drawn to the other side.

The Witchmaster lowered himself to the floor, letting his legs dangle over the sheer fall. "The Yunwi Amayinehi. They're the Little Water-Dwelling People. They frequent the rivers and creeks, but I thought we might see some near the Cauldron pool."

"Water fairies?"

"They are themselves, the Yunwi Amayinehi. Though I think they are sometimes mischievous, like Old World fairies."

From this end of the cavern, they looked like lithe children—perhaps Cherokee—except for their size and the waves of blue and green that occasionally passed over them like shadows. As the band of figures carried their burdens to the highest balcony, the singer was revealed. She glowed in the midst of the blossoms, filaments of burning hair floating about her head.

"What's that one?"

"The Yunwi Usdi? That's the term for one of the Yunwi Tsunsdi, a Little Person; in the chronicles of the Masters, it's written that they appear in different aspects. I didn't have a guess what that meant until now. Maybe the Tunnel Dweller sometimes resembles a small human, but at other times appears as an otherworldly figure of light. Maybe in a third aspect, the being comes to heal and console in the shape of a firefly. Maybe." He paused, gaze riveted on the Yunwi Usdi.

Having tossed the blossoms from their baskets into the water, the Water Dwellers and the Yunwi Usdi filed back through the door.

"Let's go." The Witchmaster swung his feet onto firm ground and stood. "And remember, when we reach the founts, don't glance at the flames in the Uktena's crown."

Ingledove took his outstretched hand and was hoisted to her feet. "What does the Uktena look like?"

"I've never seen one, but there are strange stories about the diadem on its head. Some Adantan storytellers call the beast a wyrm. And some a water snake. Some say a salamander—a giant hellbender. We'll know soon."

"I wonder—is Malia the snake who can look at the star? Is the Uktena evil?"

Jarrett lifted an eyebrow. "Evil? No. Some say that it is the same as the double-mailed Leviathan. The Book of Job tells of a bright-waked monster so large that its motions make the sea boil like a pot. That account says that he fears nothing in the whole earth. Yet for the Maker, he is as tame as a bird on a leash. He is described as the world's dragon who flashes with fire and has a proud, indifferent heart.

"Whatever he is, we need to find him. Nothing good is ever lost in the founts, and new life is always being tossed onto the shores. So it's said. Your brother can be healed there. He can go home as fit as before, if we reach the roots of the mountains in time."

They gathered strewn possessions, leaving the site tidy in case the Little People chose to pass that way. The Witchmaster had decided that they should travel with the least weight possible, and so they left the warm bags, most of what was left of the food, and even some of the linen bandages and medicines. Filling a small sack, he lashed it onto his woven belt. He had already fastened on the sword, along with the child's blowgun and bag of silver-tipped darts. After some hesitation, he gave the girl a dagger, showing her how to grip the handle and strike, helping her fasten the scabbard set with moonstones to her sash. Only when they were ready did he stoop next to Lang and lay a hand on his forehead and peel back the shirt to inspect the wound, seething with fireflies of silver and amethyst.

"Maybe he is the one who can look at the star," Ingledove said slowly.

Jarrett waited for her to explain, his fingers on the rapid pulse at the sleeper's wrist.

"It's the bites. He's blue from her venom. A part of Malia's there, inside him. And he's different—not becoming like her, but altered because of her." She hesitated, pondering the mystery of her brother's change. "I was afraid at first that she would kill him. Then later I thought he might become snake-like, and that would be worse. But perhaps he can look at the star because his blood is running cold and venomous. Anyway, he spends most of his waking time playing with the fireflies, so I can't see him hiding his face from a sparkling light. We'd have to bandage his eyes, I suppose."

"I don't know," he said; "it hadn't occurred to me that he might be able to see the Uktena, which may have much greater power to heal than the Little People. The founts where he lives are wholesome, and it may be that he is a life giver. The Tellers usually talk about the risk in coming close to an Uktena, but those are mostly stories of hunters who wanted to steal the prize of an Ulunsuti for themselves. Whether it's a danger or a chance well taken may become clear." He smiled slightly. "You may be young, but you're a fine companion for a witchmaster."

Her face flushed, and she stepped into the cloud of droplets that was sending a fine pattering rain across the upper floor.

Once on the eastern staircase, Jarrett lapsed into watchfulness and silence, the blowgun in his right hand. After the highest level, no further tunnels led to the stairs, but there were crevices and irregular holes where something might be biding its time. Only once did he let a succession of darts fly into a gap in the wall. They heard a prolonged hiss and then a slithering noise, dying away.

It was not the stress of expecting an attack that was their greatest difficulty; it was getting Lang to navigate the stairs. He clung to the rail, passing with difficulty to the next lower step as though impaired. The act seemed infinitely harder for him than the long hike through the tunnels, though the fireflies stayed loyal to him and kept his interest with their occasional antics—a soloist squeaking and somersaulting through the air in a sudden loss of control, a trio humming a microscopic song from atop his nose, or a whole choir sweeping back and forth like a singing school of minnows.

They want him to live, Ingledove thought, feeling strangely divided between a grief-stricken fear for her brother and the pleasure of seeing the silver creatures dance him down the stairs. For him they were willing to be foolish and silly, it seemed, to do whatever they could, however absurd, to keep him awake and moving. His attention often wandered from them to the many-stranded streams that merrily tumbled from step to step and made the smooth surface treacherous.

He slipped three times on the journey, once knocking his sister off her feet, so that together they rolled six or seven steps until Jarrett was able to halt their fall.

They had to stop and rest at the hairpin curves of the staircase, letting Lang catch his breath, and by the time they reached the sharp lowermost turns his legs were trembling. Close to the bottom he had to be frogmarched between the other two, his head flopping from side to side, though he regained some interest in his surroundings when another company of Little People emerged from the door above the western stairs.

These were glowing figures who sang as they moved swiftly along the staircase, wreaths in their hands.

Ingledove turned to Lang, feeling a sudden fright that the flowery hoops were neither crowns nor gifts to the Uktena but funerary offerings. At that moment, swaying as he held on to the rail, he looked entirely otherworldly. Blue shadows had crept under his eyes, and the rest of his countenance was drained and white. Fresh silver had collected on his chest and at his temples. Nothing about him reminded her of her brother. Nothing reassured her that life for him would ever be as it had been. Only his profile and form remained as ghosts of his old self, like the shed case of a cicada still stuck to a pine tree.

SNAKE AND STAR

At twilight the cavern blushed to carmine, and fireflies rose to the ceiling and drifted overhead like traveling stars. Ingledove knelt by the water, chafing her brother's cold hands between her own warm ones, Jarrett's words of an hour before etched in her mind: *It's not just Lang; it's not just me or you or anyone. Beings like the Lamia put all of Adantis in peril. And if Adantis is lost, the whole of Earth might as well be lost. I've been in the world; I've crossed the seas and seen the towers and spires of the past. I've visited storehouses of treasure and libraries of rare knowledge pillaged from foreign kingdoms that are now no more. But Adantis is the soul of the planet, where all that once seemed a dark or a shining mystery has survived and flourished. Outside its borders the people think that they've mastered the zones of hemisphere and mind, mapped and stored life's innermost secrets. They're wrong—there's meaning free of their fiddling. There's a numinous, springing life that will forever be beyond the grasp of*

machines and men. Others have frittered away their souls and bartered what matters for the toys of the age. Not here in Adantis, where a soul lends light to each human face and where the rivers and mountains are still alive and restless with inexplicable beings. That's why it was worth laying my childhood on the altar of the Witchmaster; that's why I'm still guardian of Adantis. And I think it's why you were chosen by the Ulunsuti. Because it's in you to know and be known by this realm. To become someone who belongs here more than anywhere else.

The Little People were singing in high, tremulous voices that echoed through the chamber. Across the shallow water that now seemed a pool and now a river, the shining figures waded, setting bright-hearted lilies on the surface. Ingledove looked down at her brother. He was waxen, the blue smudges under his eyes growing darker in the transparent skin. Only a careful long gaze showed her that he still breathed. The flicker of a nostril, the faint rise of the chest under the breastplate of silver: that was all.

He's going to die, she realized. *He's floating away, and he'll never tease and chase me through the Copper Baron's arbors of roses and grapes, and no one else in the whole world will talk to me about Marm's funny ways and the old times on Hazel Creek. Those things will be drowned a second time, never to be seen again. We'll never play a last-minute childish game of hide-and-seek as the constellations are laid out in the sky and Danagasta calls us to come inside.*

Such thoughts were a foretaste of mourning. Yet the breaking of the chain between them was mixed so indissolubly with the lights sailing under the tinted roof and the figures of the starry Yunwi Tsunsdi skipping in the low waters and kicking up rainbowed spray that she felt heartbreak to be leavened with delight.

Briefly the image of two serpents spiraled around the caduceus—an image on a book at school—came into her mind. The history teacher kept his favorite books in an old-fashioned case with doors that locked with an iron key: *The Story of Medicine* was the one with a staff stamped in gilt on the cover. It was the fabled wand of the messenger god, Hermes, the silver-tongued and silver-heeled.

The Tunnel Makers, the dying Lang, the lost world of Hazel Creek, the two serpents, twisted together . . . As Ingledove wondered at the curious tangle of her thoughts and feelings, the strange, irrational gladness increased, so that she could hardly think of anything but the fount of exultation rising within her.

What is it—what is this? she thought. *What is this joyfulness, this glory inside like an upside-down rain of silver fireflies?*

From the depths of the cavern, something resembling a burning cloud was blown forward, riding on foaming breakers. "What is it?" she whispered, staring intently. *It was none of the Little People. It was not Malia, striding the waves, for she had never shone like the sun.* She shielded her eyes from the piercing rays as she heard Jarrett shout a warning. *It was the Uktena.* And for the first time in more than an hour, Lang shifted his head and gazed across the pool, now turbulent with currents that erupted from every point of the compass. He stared at the Uktena and did not die, and white stars were reflected in his eyes. Hand blotting out the spears of flame that streaked from its brow and made the waters coruscate, Ingledove glimpsed a body spotted and ring-straked, different from that of any being she had ever seen. It was massive, fell, and monstrous, and yet managed to be both strange and comical. Armored like a flamboyant artichoke, leaf over plated leaf shielded its mysterious heart. The creature was plump, its bulk decked with a wild motley of tints. Laughing, the Tunnel Dwellers danced around the tremendous trunk, and Ingledove realized that this chamber at the bottom of the world had been dug so large because the Uktena needed room to sport and play. His dragonish bulk towered from the water, the iridescent skin shattering reflected silver into many sparks. Floodgates sluiced from his sides as the Little People sang and wove a circlet of flowers. The Uktena bent to their urgings, and lilies settled around his behemoth throat. When Ingledove tried to spy the face, she found that the immense star atop the head seemed to obliterate the upper part of the serpent's body with its blaze of fire. She caught sight only of a glistening green frill on the neck.

Was this the ancient Leviathan, swaying to the angelic music of the Yunwi Tsunsdi? Engrossed, she had let Lang's hand drop. As if jerked back from the edge of sleep, she jumped, startled by the sound of her name. Her brother's eyes were unseeing, his skin looking more ghostly and translucent than ever. Had he called to her?

"Don't go," she whispered, stroking the spray-soaked hair from his forehead.

But it hadn't been he who had spoken. She could still hear the syllables vibrating in the air, and as she stumbled to her feet, she saw that Jarrett must have yelled the name in warning.

The Lamia was approaching, no snake-tailed cross between

species forbidden to one another and no white serpent but a woman. Smiling, Malia sidled closer, circling the Witchmaster, moving nearer to where Lang lay with his eyes fixed on nothingness. She was whispering *Jarrett, Jarrett, Jarrett,* and the girl remembered that the name was not his true one and was only a sign to point the way.

Hands out as if to protect her brother, she watched the foes wheel and shift to face each other. The Witchmaster had raised the sword; in his other hand, garlanded with wild parsnip, was a cross moline that had hung near the Ulunsuti, the ends of both the upright and the transverse cast in the shape of ravens' heads. His arms were coated with silver. She strained to catch his words, shouted over the flooding song of the Dwellers:

Sge!

I step over your soul:
Your kind is Lamiae.
You have no clan, no home,
Your name is Malia,
Miala, Aliam, Lamai,
Amlia, Liama, Maial—
Words wholly blue.

Sge!

I cast you into the uplands
Of the Darkening Land,
Into the black house

Where things without souls
Not born of the Maker
Are frustrate forever,
Banished from Earth.

The circlet of foliage on his head shimmered with the borrowed light of fireflies, and more of them swirled downward and spangled his shoulders and hair. The cross moline and the pommel of the sword became massy with swarms of the insects.

Malia cringed, shuddering as a deep indigo surged under the mesh of fine diamond plates that made up her false human skin. She appeared about to faint, collapsing onto her knees and catching herself with an outstretched hand before she collected herself once more, rising with a queer undulating motion. Although weakened, she drew closer, striking suddenly, knocking the sword from the young man's grasp with powerful blows. The weapon clanged against stone.

Ingledove cried out but saw that the Lamia was injured, her arm bleeding a dark blue fluid. Feeling for the sheath of moonstones at her waist, she slid the blade free.

Malia seemed not to notice her wounds. She hesitated, glancing at the cross moline and whispering coaxingly. Jarrett reached a hand behind him, toward his companion, who leaped across her brother's body and flew to press the dagger's handle against his palm. As the girl retreated, the Lamia watched, her head trembling, her eyes becoming slits, her opaque throat going blue with a flush like ink spreading through damp paper. Then a smile crawled across her face once more, and her voice sweetened, though the Witchmaster kept on reciting the sacred formulas against her. Even when she deflected the dagger with one muscular flick of her arm as he drove it toward her breast, the Lamia's lips were upturned.

Ingledove crept closer, a fear growing in her that Malia was too strong, that Jarrett had underestimated the monster's uncanny strength. Though her lithe body shook under the onslaught of his words, she no longer fell back. That he had other abilities, other means to best evil, the girl had no doubt. Yet he seemed to be weakening, his gaze bound to the wide-set eyes, his chants faltering. The dagger and the cross moline dropped from his grasp.

"Yes, yesss, yessss—"

The words were a hiss, the tongue against her teeth, and the Lamia gave out a low, gurgling laugh as she seized and pulled the young man toward her, as if she would kiss him. Like a fledgling lured by a snake, he appeared fascinated by the swaying body and seemed to yield his will to her.

Fear was the pyre on which Ingledove burned, her hand reaching out to help. But she was too far away and lacked a weapon. Then, without thinking, she shouted: "Remember the Ulunsuti—remember what you saw in the stone—remember *me*."

He heard, his face half turning, bewildered. But Malia had pinioned him in her arms. Suddenly Ingledove heard the ringing of a bell, its high-pitched reverberation cutting through the song of the Yunwi Tsunsdi, which had shrilled to fever pitch as they frisked about the Uktena. Pressing hands over her ears, she squeezed her eyes shut: when she opened them again, she saw the lower parts of the Lamia transformed. The serpent's tail gripped the young man's legs as the two of them heaved back and forth on the very rim of the pool. She could hear the sacred words, forced out.

Jarrett groped behind him with his hand, but Malia swept the dagger away with one switch of her muscular tail. It was hurled end over end across the water and into the pool.

But there was still the sword, lying out of reach on the other side of the wrestling pair. The loops of Malia's body corkscrewed around her prey and curled over the floor, a dangerous barrier.

There was only one way. The girl stepped into the frothy current, the Little People's flowers catching at her legs. Something about the cavern had changed while her attention had been elsewhere. As she waded the pool, veering well away from the Lamia, transparent minnows ricocheted from her ankles. A tangle of jeweled water snakes made a glittering mesh no larger than a woman's hand. Tadpoles and tiny frogs and turtles the size of a coin bobbled in the rush of waters. Little furballs scuttled along the rim: rabbits and minks and mice in their first downy plush. Birds barely able to fly skittered over the drink, toppling when they landed. Moving farther from shore, she sensed the nodding head crowned with the Ulunsuti.

"Please let me pass, fearless Uktena of the founts," she called, dipping her cupped fingers into the waves.

A sound like a thunderous purr and the laughter of the Little People came in reply. She came to a mirrored shape, broken into stars and colorful fragments by the rocking water, and half expected a prophetic image to form on the waves. Even shivered into bits, there was something blithe and joyful about the monster's reflection that made her pause.

Don't look at the star in the crown; keep moving, she told herself.

The low banks were before her; she climbed out quickly, her pants shedding water. She heard the sharp tinkling of the bell again, signaling like the rattle of a snake about to strike. With one desperate glance at the figures struggling on the cavern floor, she dashed forward to retrieve the sword, slipping on a glaze of moisture and hurling herself toward the hilt just as the needle-sharp teeth of the Lamia pierced her heel.

"Uktena, help me!" she cried out, gripping the pommel.

Her foot suddenly icy, she turned and saw the coils of snake as high as Jarrett's chest, a sheath of scales rising to shield the woman's breasts, the eyes narrowing, the tongue darting. Malia laughed without mirth, teeth showing sharp and curved when they grazed the Witchmaster's neck.

There was blood on his shirt.

"Sssilly child, he is lamian flessh. Ssssweet flesssh."

With these words, the Lamia's entire aspect altered, so that there was nothing but a blunt reptilian head on the white rope of body, marred by sunbursts of blue that meant wounds. She bent to caress Jarrett's face, and then bit his neck.

Ingledove collapsed, the sword ringing its challenge to the ground. The whole of her right leg was numb. Strange tendrils of frost were unfurling inside her gut and winding about her heart. Already they were climbing into her very thoughts. Slow, slow, slow. She would be next, for the Lamia would not blink at murdering a girl. And even if the Uktena helped them, it would be too late. She knew it. They were a matched pair—she and the great dragon-worm, both as slow as figures met in dreams.

The Lamia opened her eyes and crooked her lips, letting out a few notes before returning to her meal, shutting her lids in pleasure. *Get up! Gimp!* The girl's thoughts were furious, demanding, cruel. Grasping the sword again, she pushed herself onto her knees, to her feet. Her head swiveled awkwardly; the Uktena was swimming ponderously in their direction. The singing of the luminous Water Dwellers swelled again, battering her ears, a waterfall of melody in which she longed to swoon and be lost. Everything was sluggish but enormously intense. Even from this distance she could see the faint pulse of the heart in Lang's body, the blue veins bearing venom within his transparent skin. The angle of Jarrett's neck made it seem broken, and she wondered with dread whether or not she was already too late. Using the sword as a cane, she inched forward to where Malia crouched to drink her fill. Amused by the pitiful efforts, the snake rose drunkenly.

Starlight slid over the scene. As if alerted to danger, the reptilian nostrils widened. With the ease of long practice, the serpent flung the Witchmaster away in one muscular thrust and reared back to strike while Ingledove hoisted the sword with difficulty, gripping it with cold fingers. She could not move this awkward new self, veined in ice, as she wished; yet when she stumbled, plunging forward, she drove blade, hilt, and hands through the serpent's body until the point met stone. The air rippled with light, and the songs of the Yunwi Tsunsdi flared to crescendo as the white snake's head, like a bud on a stem, blossomed—not into flower but into flame. It raised a flickering mane along her spine and gyred about her body, consuming flesh. Ingledove rolled clumsily away. A cloud of oily blue droplets hung in the air, drifting over the waves. All

the volatile rage deep in the Lamia seemed to kindle sponta-
neously, the bone fire incinerating the snake in her own skin.
The outburst roared and then abruptly died, leaving smoldering skin and crumbling vertebrae. In another moment there
was no evidence of the snake except piles of white silt that
were slowly melting into the air.

Ingledove lay on the floor moaning, her legs and torso
blackened. Although the consuming storm had passed, she
still blazed in an agony that had scooped up and devoured her.
She could have survived Malia's poison, but she couldn't out-
live this fire.

The Witchmaster crawled toward her. Though she saw
him, it made no difference. Nor could she feel anything for
her brother except despair: he was dead, or else so very close to
death that she could no longer detect a faint pulse of life, even
with this magical venom flooding her veins and giving her a
vision beyond human sight. She would go with him, and the
hurt would end. Would they meet the Lamia again in the
Darkening Land? She did not know, but she felt terrible calm
about what was to come.

"Don't die." Jarrett slipped his arm under her neck. His eyes
were feverish, his voice hoarse. "Ingledove. Don't give up. We
were intended for each other before the worlds began."

But she was past the caring, past knowing anything but the
pain of burnt sacrifice in which she was forced to live what
could not be endured. Her head slid along his arm until she
glimpsed the pool, a pitiful liquid that could never drench the
wildfire in her limbs. And then she saw the Uktena approaching like a ring-straked cloud on the water.

"Don't look," the Master said, his words slurred.

It was the only time that she spoke while she lay on the cavern floor. Resolution and sacrifice were hers, and the knowledge that springs forth from them. Her voice was sibylline, and a mastery more wise than his was in her mouth: "Star," she said; "snake can see star."

She stared into the immense face that was neither kind nor unkind, good nor bad, only itself—a lolling jaw armed with blunt teeth, round nostrils, parti-colored eyes, and an upright comb on the crest, into which was set the dazzling sun of the Ulunsuti. In the brief time that she gazed freely into its depths, she forgot her suffering and saw the world and Adantis, the beginning of things and the end, the gifts of the Giver that had been reserved for her alone, and the life she would lead—where it was to go, and with whom it would be spent, the grief and pity and joy in it. She saw, and it seemed right to her. All would be well.

And for Jarrett, it was the same.

He called to Ingledove to cover her eyes as her sight filled up with flashes from the immense transparent crown. The prismatic colors fused to white, and the two closed their eyelids because they could bear no more. Then the dragon head of the serpent bent, and the diamond star of the Ulunsuti exploded like a bonfire around them, and they forgot everything and were healed.

Under the Mountain Ash

They were healed by the life fountaining from the Uktena, and because they shut their eyes at the end, they were saved. Only a scar like a pale twisted ribbon remained on the Witch-master's arm, and on Ingledove's heel were two white streaks, as there were on her brother's body—a pair of comets above the heart, below the collarbone, close to a small white star.

The Uktena and the Little People had vanished into the recesses of the cave when Jarrett woke and found the girl curled by his side. Over her burned scraps of clothing one of the Yunwi Tsunsdi had thrown a glistening shawl woven to resemble thousands of fireflies. Her hand glided over its rainbowed surface as she opened her eyes.

"I thought . . ."

"You thought wrong," he said, smiling. "You're not dead; this isn't the world to come. Already the word is blowing through the leaves and gathering like dew on Adantis: the evil thing lurking to snatch us is gone. By next spring the Tellers will be talking about how Ingledove saved the Master of Witchmasters and Adantis from the Lamia. They'll be conjuring up an Uktena like an angel, an Ulunsuti like a sword of living fire. See Lampyridae's thread? It's pointing home."

As she stood with the fabric lifted like a barrier between them, the scorched fragments of her clothes fell to the ground, and she bound the shining stuff about her body like a sarong.

Then her gaze moved to the brink of the pool, where Lang still lay motionless, though the fireflies had come and buried him in magnificence. Without a word, she and Jarrett went to him, kneeling as one by one the insects let go and sent up their small flares. In less than a minute the air around the boy's body was combed with silver trails, the creatures flowing so steadily into the air that it seemed that an endless number must have settled on the still limbs and torso. At last the torrent slowed, and Ingledove rested a hand on her brother's face.

His eyelids fluttered, lifted.

"Lang . . ."

He gave her a long look, reaching to place his hand over hers.

"Lang, Lang . . ."

"What happened?" He sat up, and the remainder of the fireflies shot into the air, though he tried to catch and keep one. "Oh—they're gone."

For a time the brother and sister sat on the margin of the pool, their feet in the lapping waves, while she told him what he had missed while lying sightless on the bank like one already dead. She was happy enough for tears, but Lang blamed himself for what had happened outside Sally's cabin, and for a long time it seemed that he would never give over regretting his part in their trouble. But Ingledove didn't listen; she was too glad to have him alive. Meanwhile the Witchmaster scoured the floor, going down on one knee at the spot where Malia had burned to powder. He bent at the waist, plucking up something white and a bright shard.

"Look what I've found." He came over and held out his hand. Strung through his fingers was a chain with a clapperless bell, burned as white as the Uktena's flood of starshine. "And this—it's a diamond-shaped scale, fired to iridescence by the Ulunsuti. Perhaps you should have them, Lang."

The boy raised a warding arm. "No," he said flatly; "I don't want any part in them."

"There's no harm to bell or scale, not now. It's said that such things, refined by flame, have the power to convey long life. They may have other virtues, opposite to those they had before—to those potencies they once held."

"You and Ingledove take them." After a moment he added in a low voice, "What would I want with a long life?"

"You might want it, another day," Jarrett told him, resting a hand on his shoulder.

The Master had a date to keep with the hungry crystal on the mountain, so they left soon afterward, passing easily along Lampyridae's thread from the Cauldron of Flowers to the door where they had placed three hands together. To Lang's sorrow, the Little People and their insects stayed out of sight, though once a firefly flew to his finger and perched there for a few minutes, its chill luminescence brighter than any ring stone.

"That must have been goodbye," he said afterward, and he was quiet for the rest of the long upward climb to the door.

In the valley another dawn was already passing away, its rosy fleece melting into white clouds. From the canopy birds were singing to the rising sun. A young weasel stole along the streambank, a minnow flapping in its mouth. Wading through wildflowers beyond the mountain door, Lang stared about him as if he'd fallen to earth from a distant star and knew nothing of this new planet.

"Look at that!" Jarrett stopped and picked a small yellow blossom from its nest. "Hello, old Master—it's getting late for loosestrife." He tucked it behind the girl's ear. "You look like an islander dressed like that, with a flower in your hair."

"Then I need some of those luminous mushrooms for a crown," she murmured. What a strange world it was, that thousands of miles away the island women might be weaving a fungal glow into their black locks! Her fingers brushed against the delicate mute bell.

"Lampyridae's garden will have melted away when we get home. No *Mycena tintinnabulum* to braid in your hair." Taking her hand, he led the way across the impetuous stream, stepping easily from stone to stone.

"Loosestrife—you know, I thought it meant that he was a troublemaker," she told him, feeling uneasy and once again too young to be wandering through the wilderness.

He laughed. "Well, I sometimes thought he was! He could bother me, anyway. But I always thought the name had something to do with the whorled leaves, somehow. I don't really know why. He never explained, and I never knew any of his other names."

The path home seemed short and pleasant, and only the

winding stair felt like something out of the adventure of the
past days. The garden of bright fungus had sunk into the
earth, to return again in a time of unrest and danger. For three
days the brother and sister visited at the house in the mountain. Lang spent his time pacing the ridgetop, never straying
far from the door, or else reading in the library, though he occasionally talked about school and what sports he would play
in the fall. For the first time he deferred to a girl's opinions,
and he thanked her for what she had done in the Cauldron of
Flowers. Occasionally he seemed out of sorts, and he would
not sit alone in the room with the Ulunsuti. He told her that
he feared the hike to Sally's cabin and on to Hazel Creek but
that he was more afraid of staying than leaving—he had a terror of that uncanny child Ild, whom the Witchmaster suspected of being spawned by Malia. His sister tried to console
him, saying that the Master would accompany them. He had
been promised three of the Messers' big horses to carry them
as far as the drowned lands. It didn't seem to calm Lang's anx-
iety, though once he admitted—they were watching a scattering of fireflies float from the twilit moss, glowing with their
ordinary summer magic—that he might return, someday, if he
had no more dreams of snakes. But the Lamia, though she had
struck deeply, was not what made him heartsore and restless.

"Sometimes it seems that I'll never have my old thought-
lessness back—that I'll always be longing to see them, and I'll
have no peace until I catch a glimpse." She didn't need to ask
what he meant by *them*. Yet she wondered what it was to him
to have put on that uncanny armor of light.

"Will my brother ever be right?" she asked Jarrett.

"Will he ever be the same, you mean?" He shook his head. "He has had a series of dreadful shocks. He can't be what he was. But he's strong, and I hope he can get over what happened and not be haunted by it."

"But will he be . . ." The girl paused, her eyes on the cloudless sky. "Will he be content?"

"Maybe not. Some seeds of longing can't help but grow, no matter what we do. He may well be a better and a greater man for having failed and suffered. Not to mention having been saved by his little sister!"

She didn't smile, and her glance traveled to the spot where his sleeve covered a ribbonlike scar.

"He'll be glad to see Danagasta and his friends." She wondered at how the direction of her own desires had come to flow so differently from Lang's. Would he be as liable to find peace without her? At first she thought not, but later told herself that she would always be a reminder of past injuries and fears.

At dusk on the third day Jarrett and Ingledove paused under the mountain ash with its persimmon-colored berries and center leaves, and she told him that she wanted to remain on the ridge and never go home again. Then he explained that she couldn't, even though she had earned the right to ask anything of him. Adantans married early, but she was far too young for the emerald ring in the drawer with the sprig of meadow rue, the feather, and her name written in violet ink. She couldn't linger, because the Master above all others in Adantis must not yield to his own desires—for in time he might be tempted to take her, still a girl, as his wife. And that might ruin the life to come they had glimpsed in the crystal.

He promised that they would meet again, although not for years.

"Then you will know your gifts. You thought that you were not brave, but you were daring when you had to be."

He would wait until she was ready, until she looked in the mirror and saw that her face had become the one she had seen in the Ulunsuti. Then, if she chose to come back to Adantis, he would be watching for her; he would know by the stone when she was approaching, and he would ride out as far as the lake to meet her. Only that morning he had seen an image of the two of them under a mountain ash, the shadow of leaves on their faces.

After the Master of Witchmasters told her these things, he bent and pressed his cheek against hers, and they stood together, arms around each other. A spire of pleasure rose in Ingledove, a thin sheer fountain of joy. And when they stepped apart, he added, "It won't be like this when we meet again. Everything will be different."

"But this is—sweet," she said.

He took her hand, examining the slender fingers as if he had never seen them before, and then raised his glance to her face.

"At my baptism," he said slowly, "I was christened with the name of *Tither Hall*. Later I gained the name *Inali*, or *Blackfox*, after a long-ago chief of the Cherokee who gave up clan revenge."

Ingledove, now knowing what it meant to yield up such secrets, placed a fingertip on his mouth, but he seized her wrist and held it pinned.

"Loosestrife made me *Talisman*, the foremost of my names."

Venus and the first star sparkled like two far-off fireflies. His eyes lifting to the cloudy procession of mountains that lapped, ridge by ridge, across Adantis and bled their color into the mystic blue of twilight, he continued, "Now you know all my names. You hold my life in your hands."

An Adantan Glossary

Like Danagasta, an Adantan can speak in different modes. While Adantans speak English, it is a language salted with Scots, Irish, English dialect, and Cherokee words. It preserves the liveliness of settlers like those who once lived along Hazel Creek, as well as an occasional grandeur that harks back to earlier times and to the King James Bible. The fragments of Cherokee that survive are close to the language of the Kituwah (kee-TOO-wah) dialect of the Eastern Band (composed of those Cherokee who escaped removal and their descendants), but the Adantan's first source for Cherokee pronunciation and meaning is James Mooney's collection of nineteenth-century texts, tales, and glossaries in *Myths of the Cherokee* (1900) and *The Sacred Formulas of the Cherokees* (1891). Even before formal publication, these writings were known to the Adantan witchmasters.

ADANTIS (ah-DAHN-tis)   "The soul place," Adantis is home to the Hidden People, the Adantans. Emigrants from Scotland, northern England, and northern Ireland mingled with remnants of the Cherokee about the time of the Trail of Tears (1838) and became the first Adantans. Hermits and runaways from many backgrounds and races were absorbed into the young nation.

ADAWEHI (ah-TAH-way-hih)   This word is used to describe either a human being or a spirit who possesses supernatural powers. If a shaman calls himself an adawehi in a sacred formula, he invokes powers of the invisible world. James Mooney writes that the "nearest equivalent is the word magician, but this falls far short of the idea conveyed by the Cherokee word. In the bible translation the word is used as the equivalent of angel or spirit" (*James Mooney's History, Myths, and Sacred Formulas of the Cherokees*, with a biographical introduction by George Ellison [Asheville, N.C.: Bright Mountain Books, 1992], p. 346 n.).

ALCOA   "As early as 1924, the Nantahala Power and Light Company, a subsidiary of Alcoa, had planned to build two hydroelectric dams on the Little Tennessee River . . . By 1930, however, Alcoa had decided that it would be more efficient to build one large dam, about 480 feet high, at Fontana." In 1941 the War Department agreed to supply Alcoa with electricity needed to produce more aluminum for the war effort in exchange for Alcoa's 15,000 acres of Little Tennessee valley land. This meant that the TVA would construct the Fontana dam, destroying the settlements along Hazel Creek (Duane Oliver, *Hazel Creek From Then Till Now* [privately printed, 1989], p. 91).

ALL-OVERS   An attack of these fine quick shivers can stem from fright, nervousness, or any perception that thrills.

BOOGER   A supernatural figure inspiring terror, such as a demon, devil, ghost, or goblin.

BRANCH-WATER PEOPLE   These are mountain people living high on the mountain "branches," or streams.

CADES COVE   The first settlers on Hazel Creek, Moses and Patience Rustin Proctor and their firstborn son, William, arrived before 1830 (Oliver, p. 8). They left the lovely rural farming community at Cades Cove, where there was a reasonably flat valley with good water.

DANAGASTA (TAH-nah-kaws-taw)   A Cherokee female name meaning "Sharp-war" or "Eager-warrior" (Mooney, p. 514).

DAUNCY   The doodlebug of Knox Messer's song is *dauncy* and *mincy*. Both words suggest fussiness about one's food to an Adantan; whereas the doodlebug appears fastidious about the courting of Sir Tal, in later verses it appears that wildmires are not fussy about their meals and, indeed, are rather fond of gobbling up doodlebugs.

DAYUHA (ta-yoo-HAH)   James Mooney recorded this word's meaning as no longer intelligible, though still used in sacred formulas.

DONEY (DOUGH-nee) or **DONEY-GAL**   Although Professors Farwell and Nicholas of Cullowhee declare in their dictionary that British sailors carried the word "to England from Spanish or Italian ports" and that it is "simply dona or donna a trifle Anglicized," many an Adantan would argue that the term "doney gal" began as a tribute to a girl of County Donegal, Ireland (*Smoky Mountain Voices*, ed. Harold F. Farwell, Jr., and J. Karl Nicholas [University Press of Kentucky, 1993]).

DOTTLE-HEADED SHUMMICKS   Idlers with brains no better than half-burned tobacco caked in a pipe bowl.

DROWNED LANDS   This refers to countryside and towns near Hazel Creek buried beneath the waters of the TVA's dam. "Fontana, Bushnell, Japan, Forney, Judson and Almond, as well as other settlements and villages, were to be covered by the lake." More than a thousand graves were moved to higher ground by the TVA (Oliver, p. 92).

DUMMERN   A woman. Other variants are *ummern, wimmern,* and *womern.* The plural form is the comical *dummerunses.*

DUNUWA (tuh-NOO-wah)   "Dunuwa appears to be an old verb, meaning 'it has penetrated,' probably referring to the tooth of the reptile" (Mooney, p. 352).

FEATHERING   To "feather into" is "to attack, as with arrows piercing to the feather" (Farwell and Nicholas).

FLANDERS   Particles of a shattered substance.

HAZEL CREEK   is often called "the back of beyond." Professor Oliver writes that "as each year passes, Hazel Creek looks more and more as it did when the first settler arrived there a century-and-a-half ago. There are signs, here and there, of previous habitation, but the forest has obliterated most of these. Only with a guide would one know where there were once farms, orchards, houses, roads, a town of over a thousand people, and a railroad that ran almost to the top of the Smokies fifteen or so miles away" (p. 100).

INADUNAI (EE-nah-tuh-NAH-ih)   In the glossary to his *Myths of the Cherokee* (1900), Mooney wrote that this name was given to " 'Going-snake,' a Cherokee chief prominent about eighty years ago. The name properly signifies that the person is 'going along in company with a snake.' "

INALI (ee-NAH-lih)   Black-fox. "Black-fox was principal chief of the Cherokee Nation in 1810" (Mooney, p. 522).

INGLEDOVE   The name is a curious one that predates this history. Daughter of the first settlers on Hazel Creek, Catherine Proctor Welch was the mother of George Welch, who married his distant cousin, Engledove Welch, born in 1871 (Oliver). Her birth marked the first use of the name *Engledove* on Hazel Creek. While its source is obscure, the name may be related to the Scots Gaelic *aingeal*, or fire, and suggest a "firebird" or a dove by the *ingle*, or hearth. Any connection through kinship or friendship to the family of "Ingledove" remains a mystery.

KEPHART, HORACE   Kephart was the author of *Our Southern Highlanders* (1913). He lived for three years on Little Fork off Sugar Fork on Hazel Creek, observing many of the area's more colorful denizens. He was an advocate for the wilderness and a friend to Adantans.

KU! (KUH!)   An outcry or exclamation.

LAMIA (LAY-mee-ah)   A fabulous creature recorded in classical mythology, the Lamia was often depicted with the body of a serpent and the head, arms, and bust of a woman.

LANG *Lang* was also an uncommon name or nickname on Hazel Creek, though Duane Oliver notes a "Lang Farley" in a photograph of loggers in the 1920s. Whether there was a connection to the Lang of this story is unknown.

LAUREL HELL While North Carolina and Tennessee settlers called mountain laurel by the name *ivy*, they called rhododendron by the name *laurel*. This confusion seems of a piece with the naming ways of Adantans and suggests that laurel and rhododendron were significant plants, their proper names best left unspoken. A very "laurely" spot is a *hell*, dense with branches.

LEVIATHAN (le-VIE-uh-thun) Does the Uktena resemble the Leviathan? Here is a glimpse of the mighty being and plaything of God in chapter 41 of the Book of Job:

15. His scales are his pride,
     shut up together as with a close seal.
19. Out of his mouth go burning lamps,
     and sparks of fire leap out.
20. Out of his nostrils goeth smoke,
     as out of a seething pot or caldron.
31. He maketh the deep to boil like a pot:
     he maketh the sea like a pot of ointment.
33. Upon earth there is not his like,
     who is made without fear.
34. He beholdeth all high things:
     he is a king over all the children of pride. (King James Bible)

LILIM CHILD (*See also* SANVI.) Lilith's demon children were the Lilim. Some of these were the snake-tailed women called Lamiae by the Greeks.

MINCY *See* DAUNCY.

MOLINE (MOH-lin)   This traditional form of cross has arms equal in length, with the ends split in half and curved back. The Adantan elaboration on the cross moline converts the resulting eight tips into the heads of ravens.

MOONEY, JAMES   While anthropologists and Native Americans have relied on the writings of Dr. Mooney, the Adantans have come to accept his *Myths of the Cherokee* and *The Sacred Formulas of the Cherokees* as sources of wisdom surpassed only by the Bible.

NUNDA SUNNA YEHI (NUHN-TAH suhn-NAH yeh-hih)   *Nunda* is sun or moon; *nunda sunna yehi* is the *nunda* of the night, or the moon.

OPHIS (AH-p'his)   A Greek word for snake or serpent—a creature linked with cunning, deception, wisdom, and the Devil.

PHASMA LAMIA (FA-sma LAY-mee-ah)   The apparition of a lamia. The Classical Lamiae fell under the rule of the goddess Hecate, who governed phantoms and witchcraft. In the likeness of a beautiful woman, a Lamia seduced young men, though in her true form she had a snaky tail instead of legs.

RAVEN   James Mooney records a Cherokee sacred formula intended to treat "ordeal" diseases in which the shaman invokes the four ravens—each associated with a cardinal point and color, as in Jarrett's chant.

RITER, DR. J. F.   Professor Oliver reports that Doc Riter was the president of Fontana Mining Corporation, which employed people living on Eagle and Hazel Creeks. After three years, he quit to devote himself to medical practice and remained in the area until 1943.

RITTER LUMBER COMPANY   From 1903 to 1928, Ritter dominated the Hazel Creek villages, built the town of Proctor, clearcut the mountains, and transformed a society based on barter and handicrafts to one based on cash (Oliver).

SANIGILAGI (SAH-nee-kee-LAW-kih)   This is Whiteside Mountain, a notable peak southeast of Franklin in Macon County, North Carolina.

SANVI, SANSANVI, SEMANGELAF (sahn-VEE, sahn-sahn-VEE, se-mahn-GEL-off)   These angels appear to Lilith in the curious Medieval Hebrew work *The Alphabet of Ben-Sira*. Lilith was the first wife of Adam, whom she cursed and fled, settling by the Red Sea. When Adam bemoaned his lot to God, the angels Sanvi, Sansanvi, and Semangelaf attempted to bring Lilith back to Eden. She cursed the three angels, preferring to mate with demons rather than return to Adam. Lilith was thought to murder children and to seduce sleeping men in order to propagate demons. The three angels made her swear subjection to their names and to their images on amulets, used to protect babies. Her bloodthirsty attitude toward infancy was said to stem from a desire for revenge—God having punished her abandonment of Adam by taking away her demon offspring.

SGE! (SKEH!)   Listen! A call to attention that opens or punctuates some of the sacred formulas of the Cherokee.

SMITH, NIMROD JARRETT   This notable mixed-race chief served in the Confederate Thomas Legion during the Civil War; he was first sergeant, Company B, Sixty-ninth North Carolina Infantry. He helped draft the first East Cherokee Constitution in 1868. In 1880 he was elected Principal Chief. Dr. Mooney gave him the highest praise for noble efforts on behalf of the Eastern Band of Cherokee: "With frequent opportunities to enrich himself at the expense of his people, he maintained his honor and died a poor man" (p. 178).

THOMAS, WILLIAM HOLLAND   Colonel W. H. Thomas or Wilusdi (wihl-oos-DEE) was the adopted son of Chief Drowning-bear. He founded the Confederate Thomas Legion and served as agent of and later Chief of the Eastern Cherokee.

TRAIL OF TEARS   In 1838 the eastern Cherokee were "removed" to Oklahoma. The treaty of New Echota had been signed by only a minority of the tribe, and most Cherokee opposed the surrender of their lands and removal. Soldiers under General Winfield Scott compelled over fifteen thousand into camps and on to Oklahoma. Sorrow, poor food supplies, and a winter foot journey through rains and cold laid the groundwork for the loss of nearly a tenth of those who set out for the West.

TUCKASEGEE (TUK-ah-SEE-jee)   In his glossary Mooney records the meaning of this river's name as lost, though Tsiksitsi (tsik-SEE-tsih) was the name of a former Cherokee settlement "about the junction of the two forks" of the Tuckasegee River above the town of Webster (Jackson County, North Carolina) and another on a branch of Brasstown Creek off the Hiwassee River in north Georgia.

TVA   *See* ALCOA. The Tennessee Valley Authority mobilized almost four thousand workers "to construct the highest dam east of the Rockies" (Oliver, p. 91).

UKTENA (ook-TAY-nah) and **ULUNSUTI** (oo-luhn-SUH-tih)   Mooney writes: "Those who know say that the Uktena is a great snake, as large around as a tree trunk, with horns on its head, and a bright, blazing crest like a diamond upon its forehead, and scales glittering like sparks of fire. It has rings or spots of color along its whole length, and can not be wounded except by shooting in the seventh spot from the head, because under this spot are its heart and its life. The blazing diamond is called *Ulunsuti*, 'Transparent,' and he who can win it may become the greatest wonder worker of the tribe, but it is worth a man's life to attempt it, for whoever is seen by the Uktena is so dazed by the bright light that he runs toward the snake instead of trying to escape" (p. 297).

WAHILI (WAH-hee-lih)   A mountain to the South.

WILDMIRE   Kephart transcribed a mountain definition of a wildmire: "Hit's a bug or a sorter insect ginerally found on pine trees. 'Bout as long as a jint o' yer thumb and thick as a quill. Got legs somethin' like a spider's.

When you come nigh one, it squirts out a streak o' pizen that hits you in the eye and burns like fire" (Farwell and Nicholas).

WITCHMASTER Settlers from Scotland, northern England, and the northern counties of Ireland brought the vocation of witchmaster across the sea. In Adantis a witchmaster is honored for spell-breaking powers and influence over wizards and magical beings long known to the Cherokee, as well as for healing abilities.

WOODSCOLT A derogatory term for a child born out of wedlock.

YUNWI AMAYINEHI (YUHN-wih ah-MAH-yih-NEH-hih) The Water-Dwellers are a race of Little People, linked with the rivers and mountain streams.

YUNWI TSUNSDI (YUHN-wih tsoon-STEE) Little People who live in mountain caves, these lovely beings are passionate about music, and Mooney declares that they are wonder workers. They often come to the aid of the lost but sometimes bewitch those who stray into their realms. The singular form is **YUNWI USDI** (YUHN-wih oos-TIH).